Praise for Dr. Cory Cohen Mysteries

"A genuine page-turner in the best sense. Her years as a psychologist have earned Ceren a look at the darkness of the psyche and human behavior. Psychologist-sleuth—Cory Cohen—is both compassionate and tough. A strong, heartfelt work from a writer we will be hearing a lot."

T. Jefferson Parker, *Edgar-winning author*

"This is a good fun thriller that packs in a whole lot of themes, in a way that doesn't clash. While being entertained, the reader is likely to get some subtle education on a number of psychological matters such as eating disorders and the effects of trauma."

Bob Rich, PhD, author*Anikó: The Stranger Who Loved Me*

"Riveting, tightly woven mystery screeches to a satisfying conclusion bringing together all the pieces of this intiguiging puzzle. A terrific whodunit spun around the dynamics of psychotherapy. This would make a terrific film."

Maryanne Raphael, Editor, *Writers World*

"Of interest not only to psychologists and patients, but to mystery fans. It has all the elements of suspense and drama : a clever plot and interesting well drawn characters."

Andrew Duggan, M.D.

"Author Sandra Ceren draws upon her thirty years of clinical work with crime victims to bring a degree of realism and accuracy that is rarely matched and never surpassed."

Midwest Book Review

"Another exciting, engrossing psychological thriller from a favorite author. The well-defined characters and international intrigue create a compelling page-turner to the very end."

Holly A. Hunt, Ph.D. psychologist, author, speaker

THE DR. CORY COHEN MYSTERIES

- *Prescription For Terror*
- *Stolen Secrets*
- *Imposter for Hire*

Learn more about Dr. Sandra L. Ceren, read blog postings, and the latest news at www.DrSandraLevyCeren.com

IMPOSTER
FOR HIRE

A DR. CORY COHEN MYSTERY

SANDRA LEVY CEREN

MODERN HISTORY PRESS

IMPOSTER FOR HIRE: A Dr. Cory Cohen Mystery
Copyright © 2012 by Sandra Levy Ceren
from the Dr. Cory Cohen Mysteries

Library of Congress Cataloging-in-Publication Data

Ceren, Sandra Levy.
  Imposter for hire : a Dr. Cory Cohen mystery / Sandra Levy Ceren.
    p. cm. -- (Dr. Cory Cohen mysteries)
  ISBN 978-1-61599-142-6 (pbk. : alk. paper) -- ISBN 978-1-61599-
144-0 (ebook)
  1. Women psychotherapists--Fiction. 2. Missing persons--Fiction. 3.
San Diego (Calif.)--Fiction. I. Title.
  PS3603.E697I47 2012
  813'.6--dc22
                                            2011048687

Distributed by Ingram Book Group (USA/CAN), Bertram's Books
(UK), Hachette Livre (FR)

Modern History Press, an imprint of
Loving Healing Press
5145 Pontiac Trail
Ann Arbor, MI 48105

Tollfree 888-761-6268
FAX 734-663-6861
info@ModernHistoryPress.com
www.ModernHistoryPress.com

Drat, the ringing phone interrupted Cory's much needed desk tidying task. When she heard Ben say, "Come right away. I need you, Cory," her annoyance turned to joy.

"What is going on, Ben?"

"Not only do I miss you, but your professional expertise will come in handy in a challenging case. All your expenses will be paid by our client at your usual hourly rate."

Thrilled for a chance to see him and grateful for the income, she arranged emergency coverage, canceled her few appointments, booked a flight to San Francisco, and a cab to Lindbergh Field. With little time left before her flight, she quickly stuffed her essentials into a carry-on, and off she went, remembering to leave her flight number on Ben's voicemail."

Settling into her seat on the plane, Cory marveled at her uncharacteristically swift response. But she was ready for a challenge and had little to keep her in San Diego. Her kids were away at college, and her practice had shriveled. Excited at the chance to work with Ben—and earn a good chuck of money in the process, she wondered if her feelings would be different when he wasn't playing her hero.

A few months ago, after a patient had disappeared and Cory had discovered her office bugged, she'd hired Ben, a private investigator to solve the crime. The chemistry between them had been incredible, but before their relationship had time to grow, he accepted an assignment out of town. Cory looked forward to his frequent calls, and now *I need you, Cory* echoed in her head.

Rain formed a diagonal pattern across the cabin windows. Cory envisioned a new career—consultant to a private investigator. The sketchy details Ben had provided were enough to spark her interest.

A woman seated next to her tried to strike up a conversation, but, eager to continue the fantasy, Cory opened a book. Turbulence jolted the plane. Her seat mate moaned.

"Imagine we're on a roller-coaster ride," Cory offered.

"I'll try. Do you live in San Francisco?" the woman asked, gripping the arm rests.

"No. San Diego. And you?"

"I… I'm not sure."

You don't need this; you're off duty, Cory told herself, shutting her eyes, but when she heard the woman gasp, she opened them.

The woman's labored breathing and ashen face glistening with sweat suggested she was in the midst of panic or a heart attack. Cory reached for her hand and signaled the flight attendant.

"Are you in pain?" Cory asked the troubled woman.

"N… no… scared," she said, her lips quivering.

"We're almost there."

The woman turned her head to look out the window, and soon her breathing slowed. The flight attendant brought her a moist towel.

"Thanks," she mumbled, clutching it to her brow.

Suddenly, the plane lurched and her cold hand grasped Cory's.

Cory needed to calm her. "This will soon pass. I know it's scary, but we'll be okay."

Finally, the turbulence stopped and a crackling sound intruded with an announcement: "This is Captain Shane. We'll be landing in fifteen minutes. Please keep your seat belts fastened and tables in an upright position. It's raining in San Francisco with ground fog, and a temperature of fifty-six degrees. Enjoy your stay."

The rain trickled down the windows. Cory looked forward to the foggy evenings to add to the mystery, intrigue, and romance of her visit.

"Mark Twain wrote he'd spent the coldest winter one summer in San Francisco," she said.

The woman nodded. "That's clever. Thanks for trying to distract me."

Cory's seatmate appeared to be somewhere near forty years old. Her silken hair was a blend of blonde and premature gray. High cheekbones and pale skin gave her a Nordic appearance. She wore a belted khaki raincoat. She kicked off her shoes and wiggled her toes—the nails painted blood red. The woman was barelegged. Her wristwatch read three hours later than Cory's, suggesting that she had traveled from the East Coast. It was cold there and Cory wondered about the absent hose.

"I'm Cory Cohen," she said to the barelegged woman.

"Ingrid Gunderson and I live in New York City," she said. "Thanks for your kindness. It isn't the turbulence that frightens me. It's something else—I'm afraid to get off this plane."

"Why?"

"I'm afraid someone will kill me."

"Who would want to kill you?" Cory asked, afraid she was on a busman's holiday with a paranoid woman, a woman who—when she'd first asked her—didn't seem to know where she lived.

"My husband. He threatened that if I left him, he'd kill me. I assure you, he meant it. And believe me, he's quite capable."

Remembering the blackened eyes, swollen mouths, and broken teeth of several women she had treated, Cory shuddered, scanning Ingrid's flawless pale face and trembling lips. She knew that in the heat of anger, batterers didn't stop to think about where to strike and often aimed for the face. Although Ingrid was slumped in her seat, Cory figured they were the same height—five-nine. If her husband was shorter, he might lash out at her body. She believed this woman was her husband's punching bag; she had the terrified look of a trapped animal—a look worn by too many women.

"I worry about covering my tracks. He's so clever, I'm afraid that he'll find me and…" Her thin hands rose to her face as she sobbed. Cory pulled out a pack of tissues from her pocket. Ingrid took one and dabbed her eyes. A wide gold wedding band was on the ring finger of her right hand, European style.

"Thank you," she mumbled. "I shouldn't be telling you this, but I've nowhere to turn—no one to confide in."

"It's okay. I'm used to it. I'm a psychologist. I've worked with battered women."

"Then I've run into a bit of good luck today."

"Do you have a plan?"

"Not long range. When we land, I'll taxi to Union Square and move into a hotel until I figure out what to do." She shivered, tightening her coat and mumbled, "I wish I could just vanish into the fog."

"There's a safe house near San Francisco. A battered women's shelter."

"I know all about that, but I'm afraid Ibraham would figure out a way to penetrate it. It would be wrong to put others in danger."

"I understand. I'm expecting to meet someone at the terminal—a private investigator. Maybe he'll have a suggestion."

"Oh dear. I hope he won't mind. It would be hard to manage without some help. I'd gladly pay for advice."

Ingrid was a typical battered woman. Feeling unworthy of someone's concern, she expected to buy it.

"It won't be necessary. You're not his client."

When the plane touched down, Ingrid struggled to her feet and had a hard time retrieving her carry-on bag from the overhead bin.

"Here, let me," Cory said, pulling down the light-weight case.

Ingrid gripped her stomach and started to double over.

"You're in pain. Should I get help?"

"No. It's passed."

"Have you seen a doctor after what happened?"

"I had no time. I rushed to the bank and withdrew my money in traveler's checks. Now I worry if he can trace them. I cashed some at the airport into kroner, but I can convert it. I'm trying to account for everything to cover my trail." She limped alongside Cory and rolled her luggage down the ramp and out the gate.

Cory scanned the area for Ben, but there was no sign of him. Her cellphone jingled. There was a voice message from Ben. He was detained in jammed traffic and advised her to hop the Airporter Shuttle to the Tuscan Inn at Fisherman's Wharf, where he would meet her as soon as possible.

"I'm sorry, Ingrid. My friend can't make it—snarled traffic. I'll grab a shuttle to the hotel."

"I'm so scared. Oh, please, do you mind if I tag along?"

"Not at all."

"Where are you staying?" Ingrid asked.

"Tuscan Inn."

"I'll try to book a room there too." They were standing in the terminal near the hotel reservation phones. Cory waited while Ingrid made a reservation under the name Greta Bloom. "I feel a tad better with you around. May I take you and your friend to dinner, tonight, please? I don't want to be by myself and it would be so lovely if I could join you," she pleaded.

Had Cory presented herself as a savior—a role she'd played all her life? At first it was with pets, later with patients. Alone and vulnerable, Ingrid clung to her like a frightened child. Knowing that most batterers carry out their threats, Cory felt sorry for her, but she had looked forward to a romantic dinner with Ben. Should she allow this desperate woman to intrude?

It's a shanda—a shame not to help a needy person, said Grandma, the voice of her conscience. But would Ben understand?

"Thanks. It'll be fine if it doesn't interfere with my friend's plans."

Outside the terminal, enveloped by thick fog, they boarded the shuttle a moment before it pulled away. Rear lights from the cars ahead guided the plodding caravan. The trip seemed interminable.

Finally they reached the hotel. Although tired from the tension, Cory agreed to meet Ingrid in the lobby for the hospitality hour after they settled in their rooms and freshened up.

Cory thought she had set the speed record for getting ready, but Ingrid won. She found her in the lobby, draining a glass of wine and nibbling a piece of cheese. She wore a low-cut white silk shirt exposing the cleavage between her ample breasts. Her black wool miniskirt showed off her long, shapely legs. Ingrid was sex personified.

The server filled Cory's glass. Within minutes, Ingrid had a refill, and caressed the stem of her glass.

Cory's neck felt stiff from frequent craning toward the hotel entrance for Ben's arrival. Why hadn't he called yet? He could have had an accident or other trouble. How worrisome to be involved with a man in a dangerous job. Perhaps that had contributed to his divorce.

"Your name is Cohen, huh?" Ingrid mused. "With your Asian features, it must be your husband's name."

"No, my father's." The name I grew up with that caused me pain when people chuckled over it.

"Now, let me see. Your mother is a gorgeous Asian woman and your father is a tall Jew. You inherited the best of each of them."

Cory smiled. "You're very observant."

When people tried to figure out her ethnic background, Cory used to feel uncomfortable, but after years on the couch and her training plus the passage of time, she had become less affected by it. Perhaps it contributed to her sensitivity to others who feel out of the mainstream. Times have changed for the better in terms of the values of many young people, who seem more accepting of racial differences.

"Well you kept your father's name, so either you are a feminist or weren't married?"

"Yes, I kept my father's name and I'm a feminist. I'm the mother of two young adults." Cory smiled thinking of Rachel and Noah, two independent people trying to make their own way in life. She was pleased Rachel's interest in children has led her towards teaching. She hoped Noah would find success as a nature photographer

"We're contemporaries, Cory. I have one child, a daughter from my first marriage. Heather's the delight of my life. She's at Princeton now. I do hope your only experience with batterers has been with patients."

"Well, I'm personally familiar with emotional battering—verbal abuse from my ex-husband, "Cory blurted, feeling comfortable with this stranger.

"Oh, Ibrahim did that to me, too. Not right away, or I'd never have married him. When we met, he pretended to care about women's rights, yet he's Jordanian. Odd, yes? Imagine a Middle-Eastern man concerned with women's rights! I believed him because he's well-educated and seemed westernized. He'd even have a drink, now and then. Before we married, I'd traveled extensively in Europe, marketing the fabrics I designed. He pretended to admire that *Ingrid's Images* was thriving..." Her eyes glazed as though she longed for the safety of her past. "Later, he forced me to quit. If I hadn't believed his threats, I'd have divorced him."

"What else attracted you?" Cory asked, swirling the dark red wine in her glass.

"Oh! I like passionate men with dark complexions and bushy mustaches. Damn man seduced me with lies! Ibraham cares no more about women's equality than any man from his part of the world—a typical male chauvinist who regards women as chattel," she said loudly. "May he rot in hell!"

People turned to stare at them and the abrupt change in Ingrid's tone surprised Cory. Fortified by wine, Ingrid signaled for another serving of liquid courage. Cory figured Ingrid was alcoholic.

"It may be safer if you didn't call attention to yourself, Ingrid."

"You're right. I'm just so bloody angry!"

"With good cause. Where did you meet Ibrahim?"

"At a social gathering of UN diplomats. He was sophisticated and well-traveled, and I was charmed. He masqueraded as a politically correct man. Not long after we married, it all changed and the violence began. Stupidly, I thought I'd provoked it because he was intensely jealous, and frankly, after a few drinks, I do become flirtatious with men."

"He battered you for that?"

"Those beatings I could accept, because I felt I deserved them, but there were others that weren't my fault. He hit me when he was frustrated--when things didn't go right for him or when I spent money on my daughter—my money, not his, mind you. She hates Ibrahim. At first, I thought she was jealous of him, but later, I realized she saw through him," she said, drumming her long manicured fingernails on the table.

"Were you ever treated for your bruises?"

"I know what you're after. Yes. My doctor suspected my husband was abusive and referred me to a psychologist. I didn't go because Ibrahim was having me followed. He would have found out and there'd be hell to pay—for me and the psychologist. You can't imagine what it feels like to be a prisoner in your marriage."

"How did you escape?"

"Today, I got lucky. That bastard usually hangs around after he hits me to make sure I won't run away, but this time he stormed out, slamming the door so hard it nearly fell from the hinges. Quickly, I booked the last available seat on a plane to Copenhagen, packed my overnighter, and stashed it in a large black plastic bag— like a sack of garbage. I wrapped myself in a shawl, sneaked out the service entrance, and fled the apartment. If his snoop saw me, he'd think I was a maid. I hopped on a bus and jumped off at the next stop."

"Sounds like you planned it well."

"You've no idea how long I've imagined it." She sighed. "I hailed a cab to the bank, then on to the airport. I needed to leave a false trail, so I arrived five minutes before flight time, hoping they'd have given my seat to Copenhagen away. They exchanged my ticket for airline coupons. I've been on quite a few flights today."

"You're very resourceful. What makes you so sure he'll find you?"

"He very powerful and has contacts everywhere. He's a diplomat. He can get away with murder in a foreign country. It's horribly unfair!" Her accent was soft and almost undetectable apart from a wheeze at the end of her sentences common to some Danes. She caught Cory glancing at the lobby entrance. "Cory, you look worried about your friend. Didn't you say he was stuck in traffic?"

"Yes, but he has a cellphone and would call if he could. I hope he's not in trouble."

"Now you have two people causing you worry: Your new friend Ingrid and your old one, the detective."

Cory felt Ingrid was trying to suck her into a friendship and had the urge to shrug her off, but she was concerned for her and found her European style attractive. She was intelligent and open, but probably alcoholic.

Ingrid peeked into the adjoining bar where piano music played, "What a difference a day makes." For her, it sure did. "It's time for a real drink and I'd like to get closer to the piano. It would cheer me."

A real drink. Oh, yes. Cory was on a busman's holiday.

"Would you join me?"

"No thanks. I'll wait here for Ben."

A few minutes later, he breezed in, a soaked raincoat draped over his shoulders. His dark hair, now matted, warm brown eyes, strong physique—Cory flew into his arms.

"It's great to see you, Cory!" He proved it with a tight hug. She inhaled his familiar, faint herbal scent mingled with the damp wool of his tweed jacket. "Sorry you had to wait. The traffic was tied up on my way to the airport, and then the fog rolled in."

"I was worried since you didn't call."

"I tried, but couldn't. Busy circuits."

"Well, you're here now. I've got a lot to tell you," she said, interlocking her fingers with his.

"Come up with me. I'm drenched. Need to wash up and change, and then we can catch up." He squeezed her hand, warming her all over.

Concerned for Ingrid, she hesitated. "Do you need me right now?"

"Not exactly."

"Well, I'll wait for you here. I'm baby-sitting a woman I met on the plane. She's in bad shape. She escaped from her battering husband today."

"I see. How much time will you need with her?"

"Very little. I know she's an intrusion, but I felt sorry for her and let her attach herself to me."

"Just like women. They make instant friends with someone they meet in the ladies room."

Cory nodded. "I think men are jealous of that."

"So where is she?"

"In the bar."

"All right. I'll be down soon," he said, pressing the elevator button.

Cory found Ingrid slumped over the counter with her eyes shut. Unsure if she was sick or drunk, Cory tried to rouse her.

"Bartender, how many drinks has she had?"

"I only served her one, a Chivas on the rocks. She sipped it, laid her head down and—*voila*!"

Ingrid opened her eyes, and darted them toward the end of the counter where a swarthy, dark haired man with furry eye-brows and matching mustache held a steaming cup of espresso. Cory caught Ingrid's cue.

"Never mind," she told the bartender loudly. "She's just tired from her trip—a photo shoot in Africa. I'd better get her husband."

The dark man stared at them and sugared his drink.

She called Ben from the lobby, explained the situation and asked him to call the woman Greta.

"I was just getting undressed, but I'll hurry down."

In a few minutes, he dashed into the bar. "Greta! Here, lean on me, dear. I'll help you." Ingrid clung to him like a wet tee shirt while Cory walked beside her, shielding her face from view.

The dark man followed them with his eyes.

"Oh, thank you," Ingrid said when the elevator door closed. Can you believe this? I thought I'd faint when I saw that man. He knows Ibrahim. If he recognized me, he'd surely tell him. That's the reason for my charade. I had to hide my face. It must be a coincidence. He surely couldn't have followed me." She gave Ben the once-over and smiled approvingly. "Oh! I must introduce myself. I'm Ingrid. Delighted to have you as a husband—even if it's just for show." She was flirtatious, all right.

"Ingrid Gunderson, this is my friend, Ben Fortuna."

"My pleasure," she said, looking as if she meant it.

"If that man is a guest here, perhaps you'd better leave as soon as possible," Cory said.

"Yes, but not now. I'm too weary and I feel safer with you next door." She slid her key into the door, turned and blew a kiss. "Goodnight, darlings. I'm going to crash. See you in the morning."

They heard her safety lock snap.

Ben followed Cory into the room. "Have you unpacked?" he asked.

"No. Why?"

"Some do-gooder called me away from taking a shower. While you put your stuff away, think about where you'd like to eat."

"Ingrid had invited us to dinner earlier, but I think she filled up on booze and forgot about it. Would you have minded?"

"Listen, sweetheart, I missed you," he said, twisting his mouth in a Humphrey Bogart imitation.

"I'm glad. And here I am." She held out her arms for him and got another hug and a bit more. "This feels so good. I'm sorry Ingrid's a bit of an intrusion. I did tell her dinner depended on my friend's plans."

"Good. She spells trouble. Aim her in a good direction and set her free. Okay?" He headed for his room. "I'll come by when I'm ready."

Unpresumptuous about their sleeping arrangements, Ben had reserved adjoining rooms. Disappointed, Cory wondered in what other ways he was old-fashioned. She heard water run next door and imagined him lathering himself in places she longed to touch.

Cory kicked off her shoes, tuned the bedside radio to a jazz station and hung up her clothes. Soon she heard a tap from Ben on the door that separated them. He was all spiffed up.

"So what's with your new pal?"

Cory filled him in.

"Too bad she can't be your patient. Which reminds me, how's the practice?"

"Bad enough for a colleague to stand outside a supermarket holding a sign that reads "Psychologist will work for food.""

He laughed. "He should make room for the gastroenterologist. His sign would read, "Will Do Colonoscopy for food.""

"Dealing with greedy health insurance companies is frustrating and time consuming. Not only have they cut our fees to a fraction of what they were, but we jump through hoops to get paid. They often deny payment even though they authorized it. If you won't practice their way, you'll have fewer patients."

The phone rang, interrupting her rant.

"Cory, I'm so sorry to disturb you, but I'm terribly frightened, "Ingrid said. "Would your detective find out if Ibrahim's friend is staying here? If he's here, I'd better duck out. I remember his name. I'll spell it—"

"Wait, I'll put Ben on." Cory resented Ingrid's intrusion, but felt ashamed of being selfish.

She glanced as Ben printed: M-o-h-a- m-m-e-d D-a-q-a-m-s-e-h. "Stay put, Ingrid," he said. "We'll call you soon." Off he went to investigate.

A quarter of an hour later, he returned and together they rapped on Ingrid's door, but didn't get an immediate response. They rattled the doorknob. "It's Cory and Ben," they shouted.

Finally she let them in.

Wearing the white terry cloth robe the hotel provided, and without her makeup, Ingrid was drained of color. Her hair was wet and tangled. She perched on the edge of the bed and Ben and Cory sat at the table.

"No one is registered here with a name that remotely sounds like the one you gave me, or who fits his description," Ben said. "The bartender recalled him because bushy eye-brows had a foreign accent and pestered him with a lot of questions about the area. What do you know about Mohammed, Ingrid?"

"Very little. He'd been to our flat a few times to see Ibrahim. I served them Turkish coffee in the study and left them alone. I don't know his position. Perhaps he's just a fellow countryman. We've never entertained him. I remembered his name because at each visit, he handed me an oversized calling card with just his name embossed. He was cordial. Stayed for about a half hour. That's all. Let's see—I recall that they didn't embrace as was Ibrahim's custom with old time friends." As Ingrid leaned forward to massage her calf muscles, the robe opened, partially exposing her breasts.

Ben turned to the window and peered out.

"Maybe I should disguise myself," Ingrid said.

"Good idea," Cory said, imagining her veiled in Arab garb.

"I'll have my lips surgically enhanced. It's quite fashionable." She pulled out the *Yellow Pages* and whistled as she ran her finger down a list of specialists. "I'll dye my hair dark and wear brown contact lenses."

Ingrid reminded Cory of a child planning a party, instead of a woman with a grave problem. When she sobered up, would she remember any of this?

"Since you're a private investigator, can you tell me how to withdraw my money without anyone finding me?" she asked. Her voice gave no hint that she was drunk.

"It's possible to transfer funds from one bank to another without anyone else learning of it, but who knows with computer data theft these days? Don't use your social security number or credit cards because they're easy to trace. Or your driver license for identification." He yawned. "Right now, I'm too beat to think about it. We'll meet you after our jog tomorrow morning. How is ten in the lobby? Okay with you, Cory?"

Cory nodded.

"We have a business appointment shortly after," he said, taking Cory's hand. They started for the door.

"While you're jogging, I'll book appointments for my hair and contact lenses," she said, smiling. To Ben she whispered something in Italian. Tempted to let her fend for herself, Cory glared at her and wondered if she realized that her seductive behavior was offensive to a woman trying to help her.

As they headed for the elevator, Ben yawned. "I'm sorry, Cory, but I'm too tired to drive through the fog again. Would you mind if we called room service tonight?"

"Good idea. Dining in is more intimate."

They ordered salads and bruschetta. By the time they finished eating and talking about past events, they had trouble keeping awake.

After parting, Cory slid into bed and drifted into a recurrent dream that she'd had in high school after a school chum had flirted with her boyfriend. She dreamed her chum had turned into a rabid female dog.

=3=

The next morning, Cory awoke in an angry mood to Ben's light tapping on the adjoining door. "Ready?"

"Fifteen minutes," she replied.

She splashed water on her face, pulled her long black hair into a ponytail and donned red sweats and running shoes. While brushing her teeth, she glanced at her pale reflection in the mirror. Yuk! The bags under her eyes were deep enough to hold coins. No matter if she looked great, Ben wouldn't be turned on, she thought, tapping on his door.

He was dressed in black sweats and a broad grin. "Come on in. Sorry I conked out so early last night. I'm used to sleeping alone, but I wished you were with me... so near and yet so far."

Well, he'd set it up that way. "Quit teasing me, Ben. I wasn't sure you were alone."

"What are you talking about?"

"Didn't you notice how seductive Ingrid was?"

"Of course. What do you take me for, Cory? Don't you think I have more sense than to go for her?" He questioned her with his eyes.

"I'm sorry, Ben."

"Actually, I found it amusing," he said.

"Why?"

"You looked jealous."

"Jealousy isn't my shtick. It happened once in high school, but not again, until now. Your inaction makes me think you're a big tease!"

"That's not my intention." He grabbed her and hugged her so tightly, she could hardly catch her breath. He released her and off they jogged. Didn't he realize she would have preferred a more intimate form of exercise? She wondered if he had a sexual problem.

Without tourists, the wharf wasn't crowded early in the morning. They dodged the workers who slapped fresh fish into huge buckets of ice. An anemic sun cast a weak yellow glow through the salty mist. Cory gazed into the harbor where pewter colored vessels matched the sky. A fresh flower stand with bright orange and pink chrysanthemums relieved the dullness of the scene.

Ben's fast jog challenged Cory to keep up. Beads of sweat moistened her brow and ran down her back. She noticed the great shape Ben was in and how much she liked his broad shoulders, firm muscles, flat stomach. Running out of steam, she slowed her pace and he followed suit.

"When do I start on your case?" she asked, breathlessly.

"Right after breakfast, and before lunch at Greens. Is that okay?"

"Perfect. What do we do about Ingrid?"

"It's not our business. We have no obligation to her. You don't even like her."

"Still, I feel we should help her."

"We already have. What more can we do?" Ben slowed to a brisk walk and although he was taller, she matched his stride.

"I guess you're right. She can carry on without us. She's a savvy woman."

They returned to the hotel to get ready for dining in her favorite city. Cory donned a navy blue wool suit, red silk blouse and comfortable shoes. With her damp, dark hair in a French knot, she felt like a sophisticated San Franciscan. Here, her Asian looks were no big deal.

She spotted Ingrid in the lobby sitting on the couch with a cup of coffee in one hand and a baguette in the other. She wore skintight jeans, a heavy wool sweater, dark glasses and voluptuous lips, artfully enhanced with a dark lip liner.

"Yo, Greta," Cory said.

"The coffee is divine here and the bread is delicious, but it's not substantial. Let's save our appetites for dinner, darlings. I've made a reservation for seven o'clock at Victor's. I hope it's satisfactory with you. You deserve a treat from me."

Ben and Cory looked at each other. "Thanks Ingrid," Ben said. "It'll work. We'll meet you here at six-thirty."

"I'm off to my appointments," she said, placing her empty cup on the table. Hopefully you won't recognize me when you see me again. Ciao." Struggling to her feet, she clutched her stomach.

"You need a physical exam," Cory said.

"I'm fine," she said, limping away.

"I thought you wanted to be free of her, Ben."

"Yes, but she wants to repay us. Besides, I've tried to get us a reservation at Victor's, but it's impossible without a lot of notice. She must have some clout."

"Well, maybe she offered a large inducement. After tonight, we probably won't see her again."

"We're here on business, Cory, and she's not part of it."

Cory poured coffee while Ben filled a plate with biscotti cookies. They settled on the couch. Out of earshot, Ben discussed his case.

"Here's the deal. Our client is separated and has filed for a divorce. She was awarded full custody of the kids—three and five years old." He dipped a biscotti into the coffee. "Her husband was given the customary visitation rights. On a routine visit, he snatched them and split to unknown parts."

Picturing the bereft mother, Cory lost her appetite and tossed the remains of her hard cookie into the trash. "I see. You have to find them and bring the kids home."

"You've got it."

"Why the divorce?"

"Allison said she couldn't take his demands."

"What kind? Sexual?"

"No. Something about her habits. We didn't go into it. I'll leave that to you. She admits he's a terrific father and a caring husband, but some kind of power struggle developed between them."

"I'm to help figure that out?"

"Yes. The poor woman is falling apart. She is very depressed. Needs a lot of emotional support. She doesn't trust therapy, but I'm sure she'll be okay with you."

Cory smiled. "Thanks for your vote of confidence."

"She's confused and now has second thoughts about the divorce, probably because of the children."

"Any idea where her husband is?"

"Abroad. He's taken his passport. She remembers having seen it before he snatched the kids. He'd left most of his belongings at their house when they separated. Probably hoped to reconcile, unlike my wife. When she split, she took everything, except the kids. Man, it was over."

"What a bummer!"

"No. A relief." He smiled. "It's been years, Cory. I'm over it."

Cory sighed. From her life and work experience, she knew that people can learn to cope, but trauma leaves its residue. "What do you know about her husband?"

"Hamid Mekenian was born in Iran of Armenian parents. Christian, not Muslim. A well educated family. Hamid went to the U.S. to a private school for his primary education. Later, he went to a university in Texas to study engineering. Did well in his studies and career. He met Allison while attending a seminar here. They had a whirlwind romance. He left a good job to come here and marry her. Now he's a private consultant under contract to oil companies."

"What kind of guy is he?"

"She says he's a terrific father and a devoted husband, but recently he had begun to find fault with her. He promised if she changed, he'd come back."

"Changed? How?"

"Like I've said, that's your job, Cory. Listen to this. He phones daily so the kids can speak with her. Same time every day."

"It sounds like emotional blackmail, Ben. The guy is desperate."

"Yes, but he's broken our law."

"What about extradition?" she asked, sipping the coffee.

"We have to find him first. That's the problem. He moves around and for obvious reasons, calls Allison from an international mobile phone.

"Can't those calls be traced?"

"He's clever, managed to block the tracing, but I'm working on it. Here's my plan. It's simple. We help her con him to return. Once here, by our law, he'd have to give the kids to her. She needs someone to be with her and help her through this."

"I'm eager to meet her. No doubt, there is much more to this than we know."

"Usually is. I wanted you here because I sense something deeply wrong with my client. Well... that's not the only reason, but, you know that."

"We don't always see the whole picture, Ben. Maybe he objected to her having her own way, which she regarded as controlling."

"Interesting," he said, refilling their coffee cups.

"When can I meet—what's her full name?"

"Allison Mattingly."

"So she didn't take her husband's name. Do you know how he reacted to that?"

"He didn't mind because she claimed it was better to retain her family name for her business. Mattingly Manor is a classy bed-and-breakfast in Sausalito, inherited from her parents. The children have a hyphenated name."

"Allison Mattingly sounds *veddy* British."

"Family has English roots, but she's a San Franciscan. Her work saves her from completely falling apart. She's scared—feels abandoned."

The grandfather clock in the lobby chimed. Ben checked his watch. "Time to see Allison," he said. "We're in San Francisco, so let's play tourist and take the cable car. We'll catch spectacular views of the Oakland Bay and Golden Gate bridges."

The popular route from Fisherman's Wharf through Chinatown to Union Square was a big attraction. By the time they strolled the few blocks to the depot, a long queue had formed. They watched workmen rotate the cable car while eager tourists garbed in shorts and cameras waited to climb aboard. Ben and Cory hopped on and squeezed together on the slatted wooden bench. The golden sun had burned off the fog, but the weather was cool. A salty breeze wafted through the open car.

"San Francisco is unique—special. I spent one of the best years of my life here," she said.

"I can imagine you in a gauze dress, love beads and sandals."

"Not quite. I was a later-day fringe hippie. No drugs. Nothing radical, but I did hang out at City Lights Bookstore."

They approached Lombard, dubbed "The Crooked-est Street in the World," all dolled up with brilliant flowers of vibrant colors to the awe of tourists.

Ben nudged Cory. "Here's our stop." He held her hand as they jumped off. They hiked uphill to a charming old Victorian house freshly painted white with a light blue trim. Potted red and pink geraniums brightened a window ledge. He cranked the antique brass doorbell, and chimes rang from deep inside the house. A pencil-thin woman in her thirties opened the door.

"Allison Mattingly, this is Doctor Cory Cohen, my associate," Ben said.

"Please come in."

Cory hesitated to step on the silk Persian carpet that graced the large planked hardwood floor at the entry and noticed that except for the sole occupant, everything in the house boasted good care.

Allison's short chestnut hair framed her drawn, sallow face. Her large brown, blood-shot eyes gave the impression she'd been crying. She wore a drab beige short sleeve dress from which her toothpick arms poked out. This woman was dangerously thin by design or depression. Given her circumstances, Cory suspected the latter.

They followed her into the living room. "Please sit down," she said, pointing to a velvet couch. "Excuse me a moment."

Allison slipped into the kitchen and returned with a teapot, cups and a tray of butter cookies. She poured tea into three delicate porcelain cups.

A huge family portrait hung on the wall above the fireplace. "Was this done recently?" Cory asked.

"Yes. Last year... before Hamid left," she replied in a flat tone.

Cory moved closer to the portrait to get a better look. Allison was thin then too, although not as drab looking. Four smiling faces. The children resembled their father, the image of the man at the bar last night!

⸗4⸗

Cory gasped. Ben shot her a glance, stared at the portrait and turned to Allison. "Does Hamid have family here?"

She slid back into the chair. "No. Why?"

"Last night we saw someone at our hotel who resembled him enough to be his twin."

"Lots of Middle Eastern men look like that," she said, in a voice as frail as her appearance.

"I suppose so," Ben replied.

"Without my children... I can't go on... much longer." She paused between phrases and combed her bony fingers through her limp hair.

"I understand. In order to help you, I must ask some personal questions," Cory said.

"Fire away. You've come well-recommended." She turned her head toward Ben.

"Although I'm a psychologist and want to support you, our goals may be different. Ben tells me his job is to help you get your kids back, but I'd like to help you figure out what's best for them. Is that acceptable?" Cory sipped the fragrant Earl Grey brew.

"Yes. My kids—they are the most important things in my world. Truly. I'll do anything for them."

"What kind of father is Hamid?"

"He's a tender-hearted dad. He loves the kids as much as I do. He's warm, affectionate... not a harsh disciplinarian. The children adore him."

"Why do you want a divorce?"

"He was obsessed with my weight," she said, hoarsely.

"Or lack of it?" Cory asked.

Allison crossed her bony ankles and stared at the floor. "That's right. He tried to fatten me up. I can't tolerate that. I'm too fat as it is. He forced me to eat, but I threw up. We constantly fought over it."

"It seems he was worried about your health. Have you always been thin?"

"I am not thin! I've been the same size since I was teenager."

"That's unusual. It's normal to grow—to get rounder. Have you been diagnosed as anorectic?"

After a long pause, she said, "Yes, when I was thirteen... but it's not true."

"What about laxatives and vomiting?"

She hesitated. "Yes. Both," she said in a monotone. "I can't allow myself to gain weight. It's disgusting."

"But not as disgusting as vomiting and diarrhea?"

Allison closed her eyes. Cory expected her to cover her ears, too, but she didn't.

"Were you depressed before Hamid took the kids?"

She opened her eyes. "Hardly a time... I wasn't depressed. Not enough to be hospitalized. Not suicidal, but really low. Now, of course, it's worse." She folded her arms over her stomach and rocked.

"Have you had treatment?"

"My parents took me to a psychiatrist for a few months, but when he asked to see them, they discontinued my sessions. They said therapy was futile."

"Kids often believe what their parents tell them—or are invested in not changing."

"My parents didn't want me to gain weight, but the school nurse pressured them, showing them medical charts indicating I was grossly underweight for my height. My teachers and school counselor thought I needed therapy for depression. I was lonely, too—until I met Hamid. For the first time in my life, I truly felt happy."

"How did you feel about being pregnant?"

"I was ashamed of my appearance."

Allison watched Cory reach for a cookie. Her expression seemed to suggest she had something up on Cory—the power to resist food.

"When do you expect his next call?" Ben asked.

"He never misses... every afternoon at one o'clock here, just before the children go to bed. He doesn't want them to feel deprived of their mother and to know he's taken them without my approval. It's a little game we play, as though things were normal. They don't understand divorce, of course." Tears rolled down her cheeks. She pulled out a handkerchief from her pocket and wiped her eyes. "They know they have a Mommy and Daddy who love them. They think they're on a holiday with Daddy, and Mommy will meet them soon." She cupped her face in her hands, wept and rocked.

Cory walked over to her and placed a hand on her shoulder. "To be separated from your children is hard, but at least they're with one of their loving parents. Do you love Hamid?"

"Truly, but I can't live with him because he's too strict with me. It's his way, or the highway! I can't stand that." Her voice rose in anger.

"If he didn't pressure you to eat, would you consider a reconcilliation?"

"Absolutely."

"Before the divorce, had you considered marital therapy?"

"He wanted to, but I thought it wouldn't work." She rubbed her thin hands together, like dry twigs, her elbow bones protruding. Allison was about five-feet-seven inches and probably weighed less than ninety pounds. She was a typical anorectic-bulimic, very difficult to treat and a possible candidate for hospitalization where she'd be tube-fed.

"I understand he wants to reconcile."

"Yes, but with conditions. Therapy, weight gain, and no vomiting." She bowed her head. "He doesn't know about... uh... the laxatives."

"Do you think he's unreasonable?"

Allison appeared to mull this over while sipping her tea, but she didn't respond.

"You've refused therapy and are willing to give up a man you love and perhaps lose your children for the sake of holding on to a distorted self-image. Does it make sense?"

"I know what I look like. I'm fat."

"That's the problem, Allison. You don't really know. You imagine."

"I—I don't understand. I'm confused."

"That's good. We've made a start."

Silently, she wept, wiping her tears with the back of her hand. "I'd like to show you the children's rooms."

They trooped down the hall past a library housing leather-bound books, and followed her to the nursery wing decorated in primary colors. Stuffed animals, toys, picture books and blocks neatly stacked on low shelves seemed forlorn, awaiting the touch of little hands. The silent uninhabited rooms formerly filled with the sounds of children, saddened Cory.

"What a lone—lovely place," Cory said, choking back tears. "Allison, please think about our conversation. We can talk more tomorrow, the same time."

"That'll be fine. Thanks."

They left Allison with her messed up self-image in her lonely house and walked for a few minutes in silence.

"Why does she hesitate when she speaks, Cory? And that monotone. "

"Depression. No energy."

He shook his head. "I have a hard time understanding why people go to such extremes—starving themselves, vomiting and laxatives."

"This obsession with thinness is crazy. Have you noticed emaciated models? Many are teens. Some women compare themselves to that standard and work hard to meet it. Driven by low self esteem, to compensate, they strive for perfection, as they see it."

"Don't they realize how awful they look?"

"It's just the opposite. It's as though they see themselves reflected in a funny house mirror that makes them look fat."

"Can they be helped?"

"It's very hard to treat because they aren't motivated. They don't accept it as their problem. Some think those who want them to change are jealous of them."

"Jealous of what?"

"Their thinness. Their ability to resist hunger. By not giving in to it as others do, it proves they have better self control and are superior. In extreme cases they die of starvation."

At the corner, the WALK signal flashed. Cory stepped off the curb as a huge truck barreled down the street. She froze, heard the brakes screech and the truck skid to a stop as Ben jerked her away.

"Phew!" she huffed, shuddering in his arms. "Thanks. These hills can be dangerous," she said—her words spilling out like an omen.

When the light changed, Ben grabbed her hand as they crossed the street. It brought Cory back to her childhood walks with Grandpa. And now, Doctor Cory Cohen, the strong, self reliant, the one Grandma regarded as the *shtarker*, had suddenly regressed to a little girl.

"Are you okay?" Ben asked.

"Yes. Thanks to you," she said, squeezing his big, comfortable hand.

"Listen. Last week Allison gave me some snapshots she'd taken of Hamid and the kids, but that family portrait—today was the first time I saw it. She must have just had it hung. I didn't know she was so skinny before Hamid left. I thought she'd recently lost her appetite."

"So did I, but her hoarse voice made me think she threw up a lot, too."

"A crappy disease!" He shook his head.

"That's for sure! She's in bad shape—may need to be tube-fed in a hospital. This is a complicated case. Hamid may be protecting his children from a very unhealthy mother. His threats are designed to help, not hurt the family. We're supposed to be her advocates, but I can justify his actions."

"I get your point, Cory, but the judge didn't award him custody. The agreement specifies he can't take them out of the state, let alone the country, without her consent."

"Maybe the judge was old-fashioned and preferred children to be raised by their mothers. Or he's a bigot with a dislike for foreigners, especially Iranians."

"Could be. Listen, Allison is financially prepared for a legal battle, but emotionally, is she strong enough to withstand it?"

"From my first impression, I think she'd vomit her guts in the process."

"That bad, huh?"

"And from what she's said, Hamid may be the better parent."

He stopped at a sidewalk cafe. "How about a cool drink?"

"Sure," she said, welcoming a repast.

"This case troubles me, Cory. I'm glad you're here."

"I hope it's not only because of my brain."

"Come on. You know how much I missed you."

She wanted him to show her.

"Are you hungry for lunch?" he asked.

Cory was hungry all right—for him.

"Well, then, let's have a cold drink here, before we start our climb."

They rested for a few minutes and drank lemonades. Fortified, they climbed the steep San Francisco streets and by the time they reached the restaurant, they needed an energy boost and a restroom.

The host led them to a table overlooking the bay. The server brought a small basket of squaw bread.

"Remember Hamid wanted therapy, but Allison resisted," Cory said.

"You think I'm on the wrong side in this case, don't you?" he asked wolfing down the bread.

"Let's reserve judgment until all the facts are in."

The server brought more bread and butter and took their orders. They agreed to save their appetites for Ingrid's dinner treat and decided on a light lunch.

"Here's how we'll work. I'll investigate Hamid and you help Allison as much as you can in the limited time you're here. How long can you stay?" There was hint of hope in his voice.

"A few weeks. I love it here and have nothing pressing in San Diego. My few patients aren't in crisis and my trusted pal Betty is minding the store."

The food arrived and they dug in.

"Quit looking at me like that, Cory," he said, sprinkling the tempting poppy seed dressing into his arugula salad.

"Why?"

"Because I'll be too embarrassed to stand up."

"That's one advantage women have over men." She reached over and poked his shoulder. "It's your salad I'm after."

He scooped up some and fed it to her. At first, she considered his gesture a test of her melting point, then realized her idea was born of frustration.

"Want to try my grilled veggies and tofu?" she asked.

"No thanks. I think you like my food better than I do yours."

"Is that true for our feelings about one another, too?" she asked, gazing into his warm brown eyes.

"Hey! What gives you that idea?"

Cory whispered, "Because you won't sleep with me."

He sighed. "I find you very desirable, Cory."

"Is that so? Well, there's time before we meet Ingrid. How shall we spend it?"

"You want me to answer that, here?" he asked, pushing his empty plate aside.

She grabbed his arm. "Oh my God! Shush, Ben. Don't turn around. The man seated behind you is the Hamid look-alike."

"This is a popular place. Think he's following us?

"I'm feeling paranoid."

"Ingrid's spooked you." He rummaged through the bread basket. "This wasn't a filling meal. I'm looking forward to tonight. Is he alone?"

"Hah, so you're curious too."

"It goes with the profession," Ben said, buttering a roll.

"I'm tempted to ask him if we know each other," she said.

"So go for it."

Mustering courage, Cory walked over to the table where the man sat alone, and said, "Excuse me, but you look familiar. Do we know each other?"

The bushy-browed, mustachioed man looked up. "I sink not. I not from here. Visit first time. You sink me other men."

"I'm sorry I've disturbed you. I hope you enjoy this wonderful city."

"You make no problem to me. Haf nice day."

Coughing to avoid a giggle, Cory returned to her seat.

"So, Cory, what did you learn?"

"That I'm a fool. I don't know what I expected. He said he's a tourist."

"Do you believe him?"

"With that accent? Of course. Ingrid said he's from Jordan. Isn't it curious that this is the second time we've seen the same guy in two days?"

Ben offered her the last roll. She shook her head.

"It's got to be a coincidence. Why would he tail us, and make it obvious?"

Ben shrugged and glanced at his watch. "Forget him. Listen, I've got a lot of work to do on Hamid. Find out if he's working abroad and where."

"Maybe he's a spy or flies on a Persian carpet."

Ben chuckled. "Listen, I'll probably have to go to Washington for a few days."

"I'll miss you." she pouted.

"Take the ferry to Sausalito. Snoop around the neighborhood and Mattingly Manor—her bed-and-breakfast."

"Wouldn't that upset her?"

"She signed a contract authorizing me or my agent to make discreet inquiries." He motioned the server for the bill and glanced at his watch. "Listen, I've got to put a move on and catch up with someone. I'll meet you at the hotel before dinner, with your sexy pal, Ingrid."

Cory's face registered disappointment.

"Listen, sweetheart, I'd rather be with you, but we'll have time later."

Ben paid the bill and they left the restaurant. "Mohammed" strolled behind them.

"Too obvious for a tail," Ben said, hailing a cab.

When they pulled out, Cory peered out the rear window and saw "Mohammed" standing at the bus stop. He appeared to be studying a map.

≈5≈

Ben dropped Cory off at the hotel and continued on his way. She settled in the room and rested her feet on the desk. She started a case file for Allison and wrote some entries. Something puzzled her. She grabbed the San Francisco phone directory, located Allison's number and called her. After numerous rings, Cory was ready to hang up when a raspy voice answered, "Hell-o, Allis-on here."

"Hi. It's Cory. Are you okay?"

"Uh... I...

"Bulimic?"

"Uh-huh."

"Do you know what triggered it?"

"I was... uh... angry at Hamid for causing this misery."

"So throwing up helps you get rid of bad feelings?"

"Yes. You must think I'm awful."

"No, but what you're doing is awful. I have some questions, but it can wait."

"No. Go ahead. I'm feeling better now," she said, weakly.

"I'd rather not talk on the phone, Allison. May I drop over for a little while?"

"I guess so."

The hotel doorman hailed a cab for her. Within minutes, she arrived at the beautiful house and cranked the old fashioned bell. Allison opened her door, clad in a multi-colored African-style caftan and Birkenstock sandals.

"This shouldn't take long, Allison," Cory said, following her into the living room.

"When you filed for divorce, did Hamid ask for custody?"

"No. He knew his work wouldn't allow him as much time with the kids as I have."

"Was he ever violent with you or the children?"

"Never."

"Have you met his friends and family?"

"No. They can't leave Iran. Occasionally he reached them from his office on Fillmore. He was afraid our phone was tapped."

"Where did he live after the separation?"

"He left for a project in the Middle East. When that finished, he worked in Texas, but he came here every other weekend to see the children and I'd stay at the Inn in Sausalito. We told the kids I had to work."

"Sounds like a good arrangement."

"Truly it was, until the time I found a note from him telling me he took them abroad and they'd come back only if I agreed to get help for—uh—my problem. It devastated me. That's when my attorney recommended Ben."

"Wouldn't it be easier to work on your problem?"

"It's his problem, not mine. I do not have an eating disorder." Cory expected her denial and knew it would frustrate her efforts. "The divorce won't be final for a few months. Maybe he'll come to his senses by then, if we don't find the children first."

"I don't understand something, Allison. Why don't you simply agree to his conditions so you can get them back?"

"I won't lie to him. I know I won't gain weight."

"There's a contradiction. You say you want your kids, but given a choice you'd rather stay emaciated?"

"I am not emaciated! I can't believe you're saying that."

"You refuse help for your illness at the expense of your family life. Your priorities are messed up. Royally!" Gazing at her sunken cheeks and her gaunt form, Cory shuddered. "Your physical condition cries out for hospitalization."

"No! You can't make me!"

For an hour, Cory hammered away at Allison's resistance, pulling out every tool of the trade, but the young mother was impenetrable. "Think about it, Allison. If you had diabetes and needed insulin, would you refuse it?"

"No," she said, covering her ears with her hands.

"Listen to me, please! You'd accept the diagnosis and treatment for one disease, but not for another. Denial is the major hurdle. The damage from anorexia is well documented and publicized, but you ignore it."

She shook her head. "No! No!"

"Okay, don't believe me, but indulge me. Pretend I'm right and you're wrong for the sake of your children. Damn it, Allison. If you love them, you won't allow yourself to die from starvation. You'd stay alive for them! Hamid wants his children to have a healthy mother. He's blackmailing you for the sake of the children."

Drained from listening to Cory's harangue, Allison's eyes glazed, as though in a trance. Then suddenly, she screeched, "Oh my God! What have I done?"

~6~

After leaving Allison's house, Cory returned to the hotel. Arriving exhausted, she dozed off. The sound of running water from the next room awakened her. She checked the time on the clock radio. Six o'clock. She raced into the bathroom, washed and dolled up and slipped into a black sheath dress, sturdy pumps and a strand of pearls. She grabbed her raincoat and purse and tapped on Ben's door. "Ready?"

"Sweetheart, I'm always ready for you."

"Yeah, sure!" Frustrated by him and his case, she hoped dinner at a grand restaurant would soften her mood, even though it meant enduring Ingrid.

They rode the elevator down to the lobby and looked for Ingrid, but she wasn't there.

"Didn't we say six-thirty, Ben?"

"Yes, but she may not be a prompt person."

"Alcoholics are unreliable. Maybe she got drunk and forgot about us. Or she picked up some guy," Cory said.

"Maybe she'll have a good excuse. Let's wait."

They plopped on the lobby couch and Cory filled him in on her return visit to Allison.

"Sounds like you made a breakthrough."

The clock chimed at six-forty-five and still no sign of Ingrid. Cory rang her room. "No answer. Maybe she thought we'd meet her at Victor's."

Ben phoned the restaurant. "She's not there and there's no reservation for Bloom, Gundersen or Cohen."

At seven-fifteen he told the hotel security man to check Ingrid's room. He explained that she wasn't well and had missed her appointment.

Expecting to find her unconscious, they followed the hotel detective upstairs and waited in the corridor for his report.

In a few minutes he came out. "No one's there. Her clothes are in the closet and her toiletries are spread out on the bathroom counter," he said.

Ben thanked him. They checked for messages, found none, and left one for her.

"Your friend is a flake, Cory."

"Perhaps. Or in trouble."

"What's your dining pleasure, sweetheart?"

"Let's find a place in North Beach. I'm in the mood for an Italian."

"Then we should find a kosher deli, because I'm in the mood for a Jew."

Cory laughed, hoping after dinner, he'd be in the mood for love.

Ben drove to the first restaurant he located that had a parking lot. "I've never eaten here and can't vouch for it," he said.

A glass of Chianti and too many crispy seeded sticks dipped in olive oil satiated Cory's appetite.

"*Mangia, mangia! Ess,*" Ben twirled a forkful of his pasta marinara and held it to her mouth.

She swallowed the pungent garlicky morsel. "Mmm. Italian birth control."

"No. It's an aphrodisiac." He smiled.

"Yeah, sure!"

They topped off dinner with cannoli for dessert then headed back to the hotel. Cory's thoughts turned to Ingrid. Where was she? Had she eaten dinner? She wasn't Cory's favorite person, but she was concerned about her. "I hope she's back by now," she said.

Ben nodded. After he pulled the car into the hotel garage, they checked at the desk. Ingrid had neither left a message, nor collected hers.

"It's too early for bed. How about walking off dinner?" he asked.

"Is this a delay tactic, Ben?"

He hesitated. "Maybe unconsciously."

"When you're ready, let's talk about it. A short stroll suits me fine for now."

They ambled along Fisherman's Wharf, their arms around each other. The evening dampness set in and Cory raised the collar of her raincoat. "I wonder what happened to Ingrid."

"Listen, Cory. She's a mature woman and not our responsibility. She made a date with us and didn't keep it. That's all. Write her off."

"That would be easy, if she hadn't told me about her husband."

"Supposing she's conned you?"

"What's her motive?"

"You're the psychologist."

"You're the detective. She didn't get much from me—a little attention, that's all."

Barking seals attracted them to the railing. Cory peered into the gray water. "Ingrid was so unsteady, she could have been run over by a truck like I nearly was, or fallen into the water. Maybe she's drowned!"

"If you're that upset, my friend's a police lieutenant here. I'll check with him."

"Can you call now?"

"My cellphone's re-charging in the room. Let's go."

They hurried back to the hotel and pressed the elevator button. The TV in the lobby flashed Ingrid's face. They stared at the screen and listened to the reporter.

> *"If anyone knows the identity of this woman, please contact the San Francisco Police Department at five-five-five-four thousand. She collapsed inside a contact lens dispensary and is in critical condition."*

Ben whistled. "Smart not to give the hospital name." As soon as they were in the elevator going up to their rooms and out of earshot of others, he made a call. "Lieutenant Johns please. Ben Fortuna here. Hi, Johnny. Listen, the woman who collapsed in the contact lens place today? Well, she's our neighbor, here at the hotel... a battered wife of a Jordanian diplomat... Yeah.... He threatened to kill her... Uh-huh... Yesterday... No... Don't allow anyone, but medical staff near her... Sure. Where?... Fine." He put the phone in his pocket. "No sense going with me. Get some rest and I'll see you in the morning."

"Maybe I can help. Why don't you want me along?"

"I have some business with him. If he needs you, he'll get in touch and I'll call when I get back. Don't wait up." He practically flew out the lobby.

Her first thought was that Ben would never go to bed with her and she'd better stop fantasizing about it. Her second thought was that she was selfish to think first of her own needs. It dawned on her that she should tell the police to contact Ingrid's daughter, Heather at Princeton.

Cory phoned the number mentioned on TV, but there was no answer. Was the office closed, or had she made a mistake? She flipped on the TV, but the announcement wasn't repeated. An inane talking heads show lulled her to sleep.

Sometime later the phone awakened her. "Hi, Cory," Ben said. "I'm at County Hospital. Ingrid's in intensive care. She lost a lot of blood from internal injuries. She had a transfusion."

"What's her condition?" Cory mumbled.

"Critical. She's in a coma."

"Oh no! That lousy husband really gave it to her! Are you okay, Ben?"

"Sure, I'm fine. Go back to sleep now. I'll catch you in the morning."

"Wait, Ben. I think Ingrid's daughter should be notified. She's a student at Princeton. Heather Gundersen or Heather Bloom, I guess." The annoyance Cory had felt for Ingrid, a woman she had known for two days had evaporated.

"I'll tell Johnny."

"I've left the latch between our rooms unlocked. If you're not too tired and there's a light under my door, come in. I'd rather not be alone."

For a long time, Cory tossed in bed, cursing the man who had hurt Ingrid. She was furious at him and at a system that allowed him to get away with it.

≈ 7 ≈

The rattle of a swiveling door knob awakened Cory the next morning.

"Room service," Ben said, placing a tray of coffee, baguettes and orange juice on the table. He perched at the edge of the bed and smoothed the ruffled hair away from Cory's face.

"Thank you." She plumped two pillows behind herself and sat up.

"When I got back, you were asleep so I didn't disturb you," he said, handing her a steaming cup of coffee.

"Must have been late."

"Uh-huh. Johnny and I did a lot of talking."

Suddenly, the possibility that Ben could be gay dawned on her, but she dismissed it. The chemistry between her and Ben was too good, but something prevented him from taking it further.

"Johnny tore Ingrid's room apart searching for her identification and came up empty. Her family should be notified of her condition. She may not make it."

"She took your advice and got rid of her ID."

"A check of DMVs across the nation showed no license issued to anyone with the names you gave me."

"Sure, Ben. How many New Yorkers have driver licenses? A car is a liability there. Couldn't they locate her daughter?

"Guess how many students named Heather attend Princeton?"

"I gave you possible family names, too." She tore off a piece of crispy baguette and popped it into her mouth.

"None of them worked."

"Hmm. How about putting an ad in the Princeton newspaper requesting Heather with a Danish mother named Ingrid Gunderson to contact him," Cory offered.

"He's probably done something like that."

"Maybe the school paper?"

"They may not even go to press in summer. Most of the students are on vacation."

"Yes, but it's a possibility. Hey, I've an idea. When we phoned Victor's, they said there was no reservation under the names I'd given. How about we go find out who didn't turn up for a seven o'clock table last evening?"

"Good thinking," he said, sipping the juice. "We'll fit it in between the hospital and Allison's. I'd better change these duds. A sweatshirt and jeans are okay for San Diego, but not for a classy San Francisco restaurant."

They finished breakfast and Ben went to get ready. Cory also dressed, deciding to put on a bit of glamour. She brushed shadow around her upper eyelids, used a bright red lipstick and loosened her long silken hair. She stepped into her gray flannel slacks, donned a white silk shirt and topped it off with a blue blazer and her shoulder purse. She knocked on Ben's door.

They chuckled as they noticed they wore similar clothes. "E.S.P., Cory," Ben said.

"You must have peeked in. We look silly. I'll change to a sweater," Cory said, turning on her heel.

"A tight one, no bra."

Cory grimaced, shook her head and went back to change without heeding him.

On the drive toward the hospital, the dread of hearing bad news about Ingrid churned Cory's stomach and increased as the ominous gray building came into view. The jangle of Ben's cellphone startled her.

Ben pulled to the side of the road. "Yeah. I see. Thanks, Johnny," he said, squeezing his eyes shut.

"What's wrong?"

"Listen. We can't see her. She's still in a coma. It doesn't look good for her."

"Oh my God!" Cory cried. "That lousy bastard will get away with it!"

"Johnny has the information you gave me about her husband, but won't contact him unless Ingrid doesn't make it."

"Damn, damn, double damn," she said, slapping the dashboard. "We've got to find her daughter."

"Listen, Cory, if you'd like to speak with Ingrid's doctor, Johnny can arrange it."

"Good idea."

Ben got back on the phone and asked his friend to call the hospital. They waited a few minutes, holding hands to comfort each other. Soon, Johnny called back.

"Jane Doe? Okay, we're on our way. Thanks."

Neither spoke during the short drive. Ben zipped into a spot in visitors' parking and they walked into the foreboding concrete gray building. Their heels echoed on the marble floor. Ben led the way to the lounge to wait for the attending physician with whom they had an appointment. They sat on chairs opposite a middle-aged couple seated on a couch, shuffling the pages of magazines on their laps. Apart from a colorful abstract framed poster, the room was furnished entirely in gray, befitting the grim atmosphere.

Shortly, a young man wearing a long white lab coat and a stethoscope wrapped around his neck breezed in and approached the middle-aged man.

"Doctor Cohen?" he asked.

The man shook his head.

Ben and Cory rose to greet him. "Excuse me, I'm Doctor Cohen," said Cory.

"Oh, I'm sorry. The detective told me to expect you, but I didn't—"

"It's okay. I'm used to it."

"I work with many women doctors, but—"

Cory understood. He had trouble associating her Jewish name with her Asian face. "This is my associate, Ben Fortuna."

The two men shook hands.

"Please follow me. We'll have privacy next door," he whispered.

They followed him into a narrow windowless room, much like a closet.

"About Jane Doe," he said. "As you know, she collapsed while crossing a busy street. She was in shock and an IV was started in the ambulance. Her hemoglobin was down to six grams. Her stomach was distended. We aspirated about two-thousand cc's of blood and had to transfuse her. We had to perform a laparotomy to find the source of the bleeding. Lucky for her, it was only a ruptured spleen. We removed it. A useless organ. She can live without it."

"Her prognosis?" Cory asked.

"Well, right now, she's out of shock, but still comatose. It's too bad there's no immediate family available."

"If I could speak with her, I'd find out how to reach her daughter at Princeton," Cory said.

"Let's hope she'll come out of the coma soon."

"Thank you for taking the time to speak with us, doctor," Cory said. She printed her mobile phone number on back of her card and handed it to him. "When she wakes up, please have someone call me."

"Certainly." He slipped the card into the pocket of his white lab coat as they left the small room. The doctor dashed down a wide corridor. Ben and Cory exited the building.

"Maybe, she'll make it," she said as they climbed into Ben's Buick.

"We're on the way to Victor's," he said, driving toward Union Square.

Ten minutes later they parked in the garage at the St. Francis Hotel, rode the elevator to the top floor and arrived at the elegant dining room.

The tall, lean, haughty maitre-de greeted them. "Sorry we're not open," he said, looking down his bird-beak nose at them.

Ben showed him his identification.

"How can I help you?" the tuxedo-clad man whispered.

"We'd like to find out who didn't show up for a reservation night before last."

"Our patrons wouldn't appreciate... "

"We aren't interested in your entire list. Just the seven o'clock no-shows. We're trying to a help a dying woman," Cory said.

"Horrors! How tragic!" He clutched his chest. "By all means, I'll help. Let's see here." He wiped his reading glasses and slipped them on, allowing them to slide to the tip of his nose. He turned the page of a large reservation book and ran a manicured fingernail down a list. "Ah! Here is. One no show. Ed Koch, once the mayor of New York. Now I remember. A last minute request, but we always accommodate celebrities."

"Do you remember if it was a woman or a man who'd called?" Ben asked.

The man paused, tugging at his earlobe. "Oh dear me! I'm really not sure," he said, placing his finger on his chin. "Ah, yes. A charming woman requested a table for three."

"You've been a big help. Thank you," Cory said.

"Sharp gal, that Ingrid," Ben said, driving away. "I'll drop you off at Allison's and meet you back at the hotel by five."

⸗8⸗

Allison greeted Cory at the door. Dressed in a colorful caftan, hammered brass jewelry, make-up and a smile, she looked exotic. The change in her appearance raised Cory's suspicion that Allison had mood swings.

"How are you today?" she asked, following Allison into the living room.

"Much better, thanks." She directed Cory to a navy velvet easy chair and took its mate opposite her.

"Are you bothered by mood changes?"

"Yes. I'm not often up, and it gets pretty grim sometimes."

"There's good medicine for that, Allison."

"Never! It isn't that bad." She filled their cups with sweet scented jasmine tea and passed a platter of muffins. "Fresh out of the oven. Banana and nut."

"Do you like to bake?"

"Oh, yes. It's one of my few pleasures, truly. All the cookies, muffins, pastries for Mattingly Manor are baked daily from my kitchen. You must come and visit my bed-and-breakfast."

Cory smiled, thinking about how Allison fit the picture of women with anorexia who enjoyed cooking and baking. Many surrounded themselves with food and worked as chefs and servers. "Thanks. I'd like that. What's perked you up?"

Allison rested her elbows on her knees. "You brought me hope, but it's hard for me to accept that others see me differently than I see myself. How can I move past that?"

"That's a great question." Cory stared at the large crucifix around Allison's neck and asked, "Do you believe in God?"

"Yes."

"That's faith. You must have faith that others tell the truth about your disease too. They want you to live."

Allison gazed at her empty lap. "But I have no symptoms of poor health. I think you're exaggerating."

Cory reached for a muffin. "When was your last physical?"

"Six weeks after Shara was born."

"About three years ago?"

She nodded.

"Have you taken your children to a pediatrician for regular exams?"

"Yes."

"Well you need regular check-ups, too. And blood work."

The young mother's eyes widened. "Why? I've told you—I'm healthy."

Allison's firmly entrenched belief was hard to shake, but like the woman who tried to force chicken soup into a dead man's mouth, Cory figured it couldn't hurt. "To prove you're malnourished. Anyway, I require my patients to have a recent physical."

Allison scooped up a muffin in her twig-like fingers and crumbled it. Sparrow-like, she poked small pieces into her mouth. "Hmm. If I told Hamid I'm in therapy, but don't want a reconciliation—at least not straight away, I'm certain he'd bring the kids back anyway."

"Seems he really wants the best for you."

"And I love him too. If only he'd leave me alone about food." She stamped her sandal-clad foot.

Here we go again, Cory thought. "That's because he loves you."

"He'd do it. I'm sure. Truly. And I wouldn't have to go through therapy."

"Psychotherapy isn't a root canal, Allison. Most patients regard it as a beneficial experience."

"But I don't want to gain weight and I'm afraid that'll happen."

"It's a possibility, Allison. My hope is that you'll come to understand why you're driven to danger and you'll change course."

She shook her head, pushing away the stray hair that fell over her cheeks.

Cory heaved a sigh, ripe with frustration. "Okay, Allison. We've tread this dead end path before. It's pointless to continue." She slung her purse over her shoulder and made for the door. "Call me if you change your mind. I'll be in town for a few more days."

"Oh, no! Please don't give up on me, Doctor Cohen."

Cory turned to face Allison. "I can't convince you. You're not ready. Hamid snatched the kids to force you to get help. That didn't work and I certainly can't top that."

Allison covered her face with her hands and sniveled. "Oh, please... I'd like you to stay."

With no intention of abandoning this sick, lonely woman, Cory said, "What's the point, Allison?"

"All right, I'll give you a chance."

Cory let a moment of silence pass, waiting for Allison to speak. "Shall I start by telling you about my parents?"

Cory returned to her seat. "First, promise me you'll have a physical as soon as possible and will authorize your doctor to send me a report." She reached for her purse, pulled out her card, wrote a note on the back, and handed it to her.

"Yes. I'll call after you leave. I'm sure you'll hear from him. His name is Doctor Peter Richard."

Cory stifled a laugh. "Are you kidding?"

"What's so funny?"

"His redundant name." Cory wondered how the doctor had coped with taunting from school-mates and whether he had considered a urology specialty, but this was no time for levity.

The puzzled expression on Allison's face led Cory to believe she was either so depressed or naïve that the remark went over her head.

"Anyway, about my parents. They're both dead. Dad had a fatal heart attack playing golf. It was almost six years ago. I was pregnant and about to tell him. Mom died from liver disease during my pregnancy with Shara."

"No wonder you didn't want to be pregnant."

"What do you mean?" She frowned. "I was afraid of getting fat."

"That was one reason. Perhaps another was that you associate pregnancy with loss."

Allison cupped her chin. "Hmm... that's an idea. Maybe there's something to this after all. I can't wait to tell Hamid. He thought it was because I was afraid of having twins. It was a big possibility since his father was a twin and his mother, too."

"Really!"

"Yes. His parents' marriage was unusual—not because marriages are arranged in their country—remember they were Christians and had their own traditions. It was odd because a pair of identical twins married another pair of identical twins."

"That is not so unusual. It makes a case for the similarity of taste between twins."

"Huh? Anyway, my parents thought it weird. At first they'd disapproved of Hamid... couldn't check his pedigree. When they found out he'd graduated with honors as a petroleum engineer and was in demand world-wide, they bragged about it to the entire country club. That embarrassed Hamid and made him angry."

Allison seemed eager to talk about her relationship with her parents and their relationship with each other. Cory noted they were a competitive couple, haughty and self-absorbed.

When Allison saw Cory to the door, they embraced. Afraid of crushing her, Cory gave the frail woman a gentle hug and reminded her to make an appointment with her doctor.

Cory started for the cable car, but her stomach rumbled. It was past lunch time so she meandered toward a shop-lined street and stopped at a small cafe.

The special of the day—falafel with minced cucumber rolled in whole wheat pita, sounded appealing. A swarthy man juicing some oranges took her order. "And a large glass of that, too, please," she said.

Seated at a small table overlooking the kitchen, she whipped out a pad and pen and scribbled notes of Allison's session.

Loud guttural voices arose from the kitchen, followed by the sound of crashing dishes. Startled, she glanced up as a man clutching a battered leather briefcase bolted out of the swinging kitchen doors and ran outside, the man Ingrid knew as Mohammed.

=9=

After the waiter served her, he dashed back to the kitchen. Surprised at running into the foreign man again, Cory concentrated on dipping the pita into tahini sauce without making a mess. Muffled sobs from the kitchen made her uncomfortable and she rushed through the meal. When the time came to pay her bill, she called out and waited a few minutes. Figuring the kitchen crisis took priority over a customer, she jingled her coins, arranging them on dollar bills on the counter and started to leave when a woman clad in a black head scarf and shapeless black abaya appeared with the check in her hand.

"That man who ran from your kitchen a little while ago looked familiar. Is his name Mohammed?"

As though watching a tennis match, her large deep-set reddened eyes darted side to side. Her thin lips formed a straight line.

"Do you speak English?" Cory asked

The woman nodded.

"You must know him. Who is he?"

The woman hesitated. "Insurance agent."

"Please tell me his name."

"I don't know. My husband deals with him."

"Would you please ask him for me?"

She pushed through the swinging door. Cory heard a harsh male voice accompanied by a metallic crash like the sound of utensils spilling to the floor.

The woman returned. "My husband tell you to go." She pointed to the exit. "Not your business."

Cory hiked back to the hotel and arrived ready to collapse. She tossed off her clothes, hopped into a steamy shower and luxuriated in bed for a much deserved free half-hour perusing the *Yellow Pages*. Having no professional contacts in northern California, she checked psychologists specializing in eating disorders, hoping for a referral to the best hospital for Allison. After calling several disconnected numbers, she slammed the book shut. She would have to depend on Allison's doctor to find the best facility and the best eating disorder specialist.

It was time to check in on her dear friend and colleague Betty who was capable of taking care of any office problem. Cory craved her warm contact, but she reached her voice mail. She had the same response to her calls to Rachel and Noah. Like most mothers separated from their children, she missed them. Frustration seemed to be the theme of her week, so far. Next she called Allison to find out if she'd phoned her doctor.

"Yes. I have a three o'clock appointment tomorrow."

"Good. Just a reminder to sign a release, so I can speak with Doctor Dick."

"Oh, you must mean Doctor Peter Richard. I promise. Thanks for the reminder," she said, seemingly oblivious to Cory's wit.

The silly jargon Cory had used was probably incomprehensible to Allison's naiveté. It reminded Cory of the time long ago when she'd worked as a clerk in a secluded resort during summer recess from high school. Exploiting her ignorance, a prankster had asked her to page Mike Hunt. Everyone who heard it had laughed except her. Years later, she'd figured it out. Allison probably had led a sheltered, lonely life, until Hamid. She probably was bankrupt in the friend department.

Cory called the hospital for an update on Ingrid's condition and learned she was still in a coma.

She donned a skirt and sweater and skipped downstairs for a newspaper. Ben was at the lobby gathering a copy of *The New York Times*. Cory picked up a copy of *The San Francisco Chronicle*.

She smiled at him, placed her hand on her hip and in her best Mae West style, mimicked, "Come up and see me sometime, big boy."

"You bet!" Ben wrapped his arm around her waist as they entered the elevator.

"I'll make some calls and get ready for dinner," he said on the way to his room. "See you soon."

"Whenever." Cory locked the door, flipped on the radio and listened to Etta James belt out the blues while she scanned the newspaper. International and national news were given short shrift and the local stuff disinterested her except for a review of the new library addition.

By the time Etta James's CD finished, Ben rapped on the door. He wore a dark navy suit and pointed to the raincoat draped over his arm. "Take yours, too. It's going to pour tonight."

"Where, to?"

"What are you in the mood for?"

"Really want to know? I'm in the mood for love."

"Later, sweetheart."

"Promises, Empty promises."

"Don't be angry. I like to take my time."

She wondered if he could be afraid of disappointing her or himself.

"I'm sorry if I'm pressuring you," Cory said.

"All right already! Want me to show you a thing or two before dinner, sweetheart?"

"No favors please."

He shook his head. "I don't like the way this is going, Cory."

"I'm joking with you, Ben. Let's keep this relationship platonic."

"Uh-uh. Too late for that." Gently, he pulled her into his arms and kissed her.

"You can't imagine how much I want you, Cory. How much I've thought about this."

"Then why haven't you—"

"I—I want to please you. It's been a long time since... "

"It's not something one forgets, Ben. It's natural."

"Yeah, but when you've got the hots for someone..."

"For Pete's sake, Ben—that's a self-fulfilling prophecy. I just want to feel close to you. It's enough for me. The mechanics are incidental." He had validated her diagnosis: performance anxiety.

"Come on, Cory. Don't patronize me."

"Shut up and kiss me, Ben."

He did, and then gave her much more than either of them had expected.

Later, they cuddled in bed and watched rain pelt the windows as Billy Eckstine crooned "Tenderly" from an old scratchy record played on the local jazz station radio. Cory felt deliciously satisfied.

"Hungry, sweetheart?"

Who needed dinner? Sweet, tender Ben was the appetizer, main course and dessert on Cory's menu, but men hunger for real food. He broke away to order room service. She hopped into the shower and came out towel-wrapped. "There. I've dressed for dinner."

"Way more attractive minus the *shmate*," he said on the way to the bathroom.

Cory smiled at his familiarity with Yiddish. Those who had lived in New York when the garment center was vibrant knew *"shmate"* meant garment. She heard the water run and Ben's baritone voice singing, "I Get a Kick out Of You." She envied his ability to carry the tune.

A knock on the door roused her from a reverie.

"Just a sec," Ben called, scrambling into his robe. He signed for the room service tray and brought it to the table.

"You look better without this," Cory said, tugging at his robe belt.

"Now?" he asked.

"No. Just kidding."

He grinned and poured Chardonnay into wine glasses.

Over chicken Marsalla he related the events of his day—the facts he'd discovered about Hamid: He'd learned several languages in the course of his family's extensive business travels. For long periods of time the family had lived in several Middle-Eastern countries. Hamid had keen interests in sociology and international relations, but to please his father he followed his profession and studied petroleum engineering at Texas A and M, where he earned advanced degrees with honors. Hamid was considered a devoted family man, intelligent and quiet. Polite and helpful to his neighbors, he related in a genial but superficial way, and was regarded as hard to get to know. None of the neighbors recalled any visitors to Allison and Hamid's house. Apart from tending to work, they were a solitary pair.

"Interesting. He married a reclusive woman and they continued a low profile lifestyle. Do you think he was hiding something, Ben?"

He shrugged. "Well, here's a hot item: The neighbors across the way saw a man resembling Hamid hanging around the neighborhood. When one of them greeted him, he froze. He's described as a little shorter than Hamid. Once, in broad daylight, the people next door caught this guy peering into Allison's windows. At first they too, thought he was Hamid, but remembered Allison saying Hamid was away. They had reported the prowler to the police, but he split before they arrived."

"Mohammed what's-his-name, Ingrid's husband's friend!" said Cory, clapping her hands. Oh! I'm afraid I was distracted and nearly forgot to tell you—I ran into him today, a few blocks from

Allison's. I'd stopped at this cafe for falafel and he flew out of the kitchen like it was on fire."

"Kicked off his job in a Middle Eastern food joint?"

"The proprietor said he was an insurance agent. When I asked if his name was Mohammed, they chased me out."

Ben was about to pour more wine in her glass, but she covered it with her hand. "No, thanks. More than one and I'll nod off."

She told him that she didn't think Allison would trick Hamid to return the kids. "She loves him. If only she'd get well."

"Yeah. If my aunt had wheels, she'd be a truck."

"You know, Ben, some insurance companies won't even pay for treatment of anorexia."

He shook his head. "It's good she can afford it. Listen, Cory, I'm having a hard time finding out where he's working abroad. The last job he had was for Pru-petrol in the Kuwait oil fields. The company is very secretive about whether he has a current contract."

"Why?"

"They claim their personnel records are confidential. Actually it suggests that he's working on a proprietary project."

"That's interesting."

"I hope you aren't bored with all this, Cory."

"Are you kidding? It wasn't just the case that brought me here."

"You haven't kept that secret."

"In personal relations, I'm an open book."

"An irresistible read." He pushed his plate aside, stood and bent down to kiss her.

=10=

At dawn the next morning, Ben took off for the nation's capital to meet with his information sources. After his twenty year stint at the FBI, his contacts in government agencies remained helpful. "One hand washes the other," he'd said. He hoped the visit would yield information about Hamid's whereabouts.

Cory had a light breakfast of juice, oatmeal and strong coffee at the hotel cafe, then hiked to Washington Square Park and joined a Tai Chi group of Asian senior citizens in their graceful exercise.

Energized, she traipsed over to City Lights Bookstore and poked around the stacks and tables. The old place was smaller than she recalled, especially compared to the huge book stores, but it had a familiar charm and a refreshing absence of hyped best sellers. She glanced at her trusty old Timex and realized she'd have to shake her *tush* to get to Allison's on time.

She hopped a street car and arrived with ten minutes to spare. She circled the block half-expecting to bump into Mohammed and wondered why he'd peered into Allison's windows.

Cory cranked the doorbell. It took Allison a long time to answer and when she opened the door, Cory gasped—struck by Allison's worsened appearance. Her gaunt, sallow face and darkened rings under her eyes suggested she'd spent a hell of a night retching.

"I'm not blaming you, Doctor Cohen, but after I made the appointment with the doctor, I felt awful. You made such a big deal of his name, I thought you'd call him before I got there to tell him to scare me."

"I'm sorry I upset you, Allison. I was confused between his first and last name. I wouldn't contact him without your signed consent. That's unethical. Be assured, your doctor will make an independent, objective judgment before he notifies me."

"I see. He can't make me gain weight, can he?"

"He can recommend it, but can't force you."

She rubbed her midsection. "Oh, this hurts so much. It's good I'm seeing him today."

"Probably badly strained from repeated forced vomiting, Allison. I hope it's nothing worse."

"Today I feel weak... no strength to bake... had to order food for my bed-and-breakfast. I truly hated to do that." She rested her forehead in her hand. "When the kids were here, sometimes they helped me, or rather pretended. They'd get out the cookie sheets and muffin tins and I'd let them stir the batter." Allison sobbed softly, pulled a handkerchief from the pocket of her gray jumper and dabbed her eyes.

"How do you spend your free time now, Allison?"

"Most of the day, I'm at the Inn. I supervise the staff. At night, I read or watch TV."

"How about friends?"

"I never really had any. Sometimes I chat with my neighbors, usually about once a week when I bring them some of my baked goods. I'll go to a different neighbor each time. Everyone's nice. They'll invite me for tea or coffee, but that's it."

"How about where you work?"

"Because I'm the boss, I keep my distance, but people are pleasant."

"Do you get lonely?"

Out came the handkerchief and with it more sobs.

"I'm sorry, Allison. I was insensitive. Of course you're lonely for your family. I meant do you yearn for close adult friendship—someone to share your thoughts and feelings?"

"I stopped wanting that. Hamid gave me all I needed... now he's gone... and the kids, too." Tears rolled down her sunken cheeks.

"Not forever, Allison."

"Oh! If only... "

"Yes. Hamid probably says that, too."

She smiled. "I believe it. We really do want to be together—a family."

"It can happen—"

"I truly want that."

"Yes. I know, Allison, but you must show him."

Confident her doctor would find her unhealthy and perhaps a candidate for tube feeding, Cory hoped Allison would accept his recommendations.

"Let's discuss your interests."

"I love to bake and to read."

"How about joining a cooking class or a book discussion group?"

She shook her head. "I don't care for groups." Allison wasn't ready to budge from her self-imposed social exile.

"Are you shy with stranger? Afraid of rejection?"

She shuffled in the chair. "Well... sometimes." Covering her face with her handkerchief, she cried. Between yesterday and today, she'd gone from a pinch of cheer to a bucket of sadness.

She excused herself and returned a few minutes later. Her shiny face appeared newly scrubbed. "Hamid will be pleased that I'm going to the doctor today. When he called yesterday, he asked me to tell you, you've made him happy with your visits to me."

"How do you feel about that?"

"Hopeful, I guess."

A good note on which to part. Cory rose from the chair. Allison frowned. *Is she disappointed at my departure?* Cory thought. "See you tomorrow at the same time, Allison?"

"Oh yes, please. And you know, this isn't as bad as I expected."

Cory had walked half way down the street from Allison's house when her thoughts were interrupted by the tapping of footsteps from behind. Gripped with fear that someone was tailing her, she slowed her pace and stepped aside, allowing two men holding hands to parade ahead.

She continued toward the shop-lined street where she had gone before, and approached the cafe where she had last seen Mohammed and wondered why he'd run from it. Had he been threatened? Who the devil was he? And why was he checking on Allison? A sign marked CLOSED was posted on the door. Cory shuddered, and headed for Chinatown.

At Grant Avenue, the main thoroughfare, a red and black pagoda style entry marked the bustling area. She headed through the busy narrow streets made narrower by produce, bric-a-brac and newspaper stands until a spicy scent of cooking led her to a noisy, crowded restaurant with a counter and a vacant swivel stool. No one appeared to be waiting, so she sat down. The server, a petite middle-aged woman, rushed about, taking orders and barking in Chinese to the chef. A master of efficiency, she kept track of who was next. She looked at Cory. "Brown rice and steamed vegetables, please."

"Good choice. Just made. New here?" she asked, filling Cory's cup with dark tea.

"Yes."

Within minutes the server placed a huge platter of ginger-and garlic-scented food in front of Cory and handed her a pair of chopsticks. "Enjoy. So good."

And it was. For fear of insulting the sweet, friendly server, Cory felt compelled to finish the dish. Solicitous, she gave Cory more attention and seemed friendlier to her than to the other customers, most of whom were Asian men or couples. "You're right. It's delicious. May I take the rest home?"

"You live near?"

"I'm visiting for a bit—at a hotel."

With a flick of her wrist, the server scooped the leftovers into a cardboard container. "Soon, you come see me again?" She placed the carton into a brown paper sack and tossed in a pair of disposable chopsticks and two fortune cookies.

"Sure." Cory smiled at her new friend. *See, Allison, it's really quite easy*, she thought.

With the warm package in hand, Cory headed for her home-away-from-home. A long line had formed at the cable car stop so she hailed a cab. The driver had an exquisite knowledge of shortcuts and they traversed between luxurious and shabby neighborhoods. Finally, he dropped her off at the hotel in time for the hospitality hour.

She stored the leftover food in the refrigerator in her room, freshened up and returned to the lobby for a glass of wine and piano music from the bar.

Swirling the ruby red liquid in the wineglass, Cory recalled the evening when she and lively Ingrid sat in the hotel lobby confiding in each other like two old friends. And now, Ingrid was fighting for her life in a grim hospital room.

Cory returned to her room, looked up the phone number for County Hospital, punched it in and learned Ingrid was still comatose. "I'd like to throttle her husband," she said to herself.

She flipped on the radio just as the phone rang.

"Hi, sweetheart," Ben said.

"Hi, big guy. How's it going?"

"Well, the plane was delayed so I missed meeting my old buddy—we were in the academy together. He was attached to the agency in New Orleans until recently. Knows a lot about oil. Listen sweetheart, I can't stop thinking about you."

Cory sighed. "You're putting a smile on my face."

"So what's on your mind?"

"Dare you to guess."

"Really! If we keep this up, our phones will smolder."

"Then I'd better change the subject. There's some good news. I convinced Allison to see her doctor."

"I knew you'd do it."

"But Ingrid's still in a coma."

"What a bummer!"

"Yeah. And another bummer is you're not here. A hard man is good to find." Cory had reverted to her old Mae West routine.

Great playmates, they sparked each other's sexual innuendoes for a few more minutes. Before signing off, Ben promised to call the next day for another romp.

A few seconds later, her phone rang again.

"Hello, Doctor Cohen, this is Doctor Richard." It's good you've sent Allison Mattingly to see me. She's remarkably underweight. I've ordered complete blood work for her first thing tomorrow, and I'll fax the results to you at your hotel."

"Thanks. Please omit her name from the report. I'll know whose it is. In the meantime, do you have any recommendations?"

"The usual. Nutritional supplements. Ensure. Two cans a day. I'm glad she's finally getting therapy. She's been depressed all the years I've known her and has refused to see anyone for it or take any medication."

"Doctor Richard, you do know that she's both anorectic and bulimic? And today she complained of stomach pain?"

"Yes. I've checked her. Her pain is most likely muscular."

"If her lab work is significant, what about hospitalization?"

"She's not the most compliant patient, but let's wait and see."

Her phone signaled another call.

"Thanks for calling, doctor." After she disconnected, a breathless voice came on:

"It's Allison. Sorry to disturb you, but I'm worried."

"The doctor?"

"That's not what's upsetting me... its Hamid... the kids. They didn't ring today. I waited and waited and now I'm frantic. This has never happened before."

"Maybe there's a mechanical problem—some glitch in the transmission."

"I don't think that's it. You see at the exact time every day he calls me at a phone booth at the Inn. It wasn't out of order on my end. If the phone he used was out of order, he'd find another."

"Maybe the phones were out in his area."

"I know something bad has happened. Truly." Allison sobbed. "I feel it in my bones. Maybe under the circumstances, he'll call me at home."

"A cellphone would be another way to reach you. Don't you have one?"

"No. I never felt the need, but now I think it's a good idea. I'd better get off now." She clicked off.

The clock radio by Cory's bed flashed 5:10 PM. It could be 1:10 AM or later in Europe. Allison had convinced her. Something was wrong.

⸗11⸗

Cory spent the night restless, thinking about Allison, about Ingrid, and that strange fellow, Mohammed. At seven in the morning, before setting out for a jog to distill her anxiety, she warmed-up and stretched her muscles.

Off she went in the cool mist, pounding the pavement of streets nearly empty of pedestrians, and headed for the wharf where she wouldn't be alone. Cold wind from the bay whipped the scarf from her head, slapping her face and tearing her eyes. She braided her hair, but it came undone. The jog was supposed to be fun not punishment. Maybe it was a poor idea running around alone, anyway. What if she ran into Mohammed again and he realized her connection to Allison? And to Ingrid, now in the hospital from an assault by her husband or someone he'd hired to do the nasty deed.

She turned back, planning to make some notes about him. Rushing into the hotel, she snatched a newspaper from the front desk, filled a container with steaming coffee and went upstairs.

She covered the Styrofoam cup with a towel to keep the contents warm, turned on the TV and joined a brief aerobics routine. Exercise helped rid the creeping anxiety that had come from Allison's call. After freshening up, Cory dressed in layers for the San Francisco climate and the climb up the hilly streets. She sipped the warm coffee, and made a few notations about Mohammed:

1. He knew Ingrid's husband, the wife-beating diplomat and had visited him in New York several times. What was he doing here? He'd claimed to be a tourist.

2. He had upset the Middle-Eastern cafe owners. Did it have anything to do with the closing of their shop?

3. He bore a striking resemblance to Hamid, but as far as Allison knew, Hamid had no family in the United States.

4. He was seen by two neighbors snooping outside her house, and had peered into her windows.

5. Apart from their Middle-Eastern backgrounds, what did Mohammed, Ibrahim and Hamid have in common?

She folded the note paper in quarters and stashed it into her carry-on, and unfurled the newspaper.

A headline caught her attention: *Iran threatens world peace.*

The article stated that Iran was involved with China in developing ballistic missiles and had contracts with Russia to produce them. Iran continued to build SCUD missiles and had a state-of-the art solid fueled rocket. The U.S. Secretary of State issued a warning about Iran's alleged persistent efforts to develop weapons of mass destruction.

Cory recalled having read an article claiming that Iran had test fired a cruise missile designed to strike ships. She knew that oil produced in Kuwait, Iraq, Bahrain and the United Arab Emirates must transit the Persian Gulf through the Strait of Hormuz. Iran could conceal mobile missile launchers in the interior of the country and fire at transiting ships. Blockage of the strait could cause oil prices to skyrocket again.

Cory recalled one of her patients, a geologist. He had gone to work in the Gulf of Mexico for one of the petroleum companies attempting to drill in dried-up wells. Frustrated by the project, he'd returned last year. He said the system using steam and water to extract the oil was tedious and anyone who discovered a better way should earn a prize, especially if he mastered an ecologically friendly method.

If Hamid, a talented petroleum engineer, developed such a system, oil production could occur off Louisiana, North Carolina and Texas. He'd be a valuable resource to the United States and a potential threat to countries whose economy was based on high-priced oil.

It wasn't a secret that Iran, the leading sponsor of worldwide terrorism, funded those efforts through oil revenue. Iran's support of fervent Islamic militants, Hezbollah, Jihad, and Hamas, whose chief target was Israel, was well known.

She turned the newspaper to the back page where an A.P. bulletin brought Iran's goal close to home:

Canada released to the United States the Saudi who was involved in the bombing of the residence complex where Americans were killed. Canadian surveillance disclosed he was in close contact with Iranian diplomats in Ottawa from the time of his arrival and was trained in and had received his orders from Iran.

Cory recalled that since the Ames affair, the CIA and the FBI unified their efforts in counterintelligence, and the FBI helped internal spy-catching. The news fueled her imagination about Mohammed, Hamid and Ibraham.

The ringing of the phone jarred her. It was Betty returning her call. Cory was eager to share her musings, but dared not.

"Anything wrong?" Betty asked.

"Does something have to be wrong for me to call you? I just missed you."

"Come on, Cory. We're too busy to call each other often when you're home, so I was surprised to hear from you."

"Good detective, Betty. Maybe you should join our team."

"So what gives?"

Cory told her about Allison's eating disorder.

"Well, you're on the right track with her. You're not known for beating around the bush. You get straight to the problem and stay with it. Way to go, Cory."

"Thanks pal."

"There's no rush to come back here, you have no new patients and no emergencies, but I miss you. Any idea when you'll finish up there?"

"As long as everything at home is stable..."

"All's quiet on the southern front, Cory. How's it going with Big Ben?"

"Big Ben sure makes my heart chime. He's great!"

"Ah! At last!"

"Yes," Cory cooed. "By the way, Betty, do you know anyone in Princeton?"

"No. Why?"

Cory told her about Ingrid.

"Are you some kind of magnet for trouble, Cory?"

"Is it my fault that this woman attached herself to me?"

"You know the answer. You like to do good deeds—*mitzvot*. I'm sorry I can't help you with this. Anyway, isn't it up to the police?"

"They haven't located Ingrid's daughter."

With no news of her own to report since the weather rarely changed much in San Diego—they chatted briefly then signed off.

Afraid to hear bad news about poor Ingrid, Cory had to force herself to call the hospital. Ingrid remained comatose. It was four days since her collapse, her surgery, and the transfusions. Ingrid still hadn't come out of it. Cory knew of cases in which people remained in a coma for a long time. Some came out of it eventually. Others did not. Damn! Ruminating about it was counterproductive, so she decided to learn more about petroleum drilling by using the Internet. Having left her laptop at the repair shop near her home, she would visit the library. She found the number in the phone directory. The recorded message said they'd open at ten, which meant she'd go there after her session with Allison. Cory hoped Allison had heard from Hamid and would keep her lab appointment.

With a couple of hours to spare before the session, she strolled toward the cable-car. Beckoned by the aroma of maple syrup wafting from a cafe, she entered. Buckwheat cakes and fresh fruit would be her treat for the day. She was directed to a table overlooking the busy street. Unlike San Diego where pedestrians were few, people hurried by as if swept by the wind that howled each time the door opened.

From the whirl of people flying by, she sized up potential terrorists, and then cautioned herself to stop her paranoia.

After polishing off three syrup-soaked pancakes, she realized vigilance had to become an essential ingredient in her life—especially when it came to food consumption. She paid the bill and ambled off to public transportation.

Cory clutched the post on the outside of the crowded cable car. Each time it lurched, she swayed, making her regret the breakfast indulgence. Imagining the food sloshing around in her stomach, she disembarked at a reasonable distance from her destination, and walked the rest of the way.

The wind had died down and the lemony sun warmed her back as she climbed Allison's quiet street. A limousine pulled up and a chauffeur opened the door for Allison, just in time for Cory to meet her.

"Oh, I'm so glad to see you, Doctor Cohen. I've just come from the lab and must grab a bite right away. I had to do a twelve hour fast. Please come in," she said unlocking the front door. "Have you had breakfast?" she asked.

"Yes, thanks, but I'll sit with you if you like."

Cory followed Allison into a cheerful breakfast room with lace curtains and flowered wallpaper. She wanted to ask Allison if she had heard from Hamid, but figured it would be better not to interrupt her while she ate.

Allison filled a bowl with dry cereal, sliced a banana on top, and poured in milk. As it snapped, crackled and popped, Cory slid opposite her into the plush booth and noticed that the design on the cushions matched the walls. The room with its polished wooden floors and fixtures felt warm and cozy. Picturing Allison's family gathered here together, Cory felt the woman's loss.

During the first couple of spoonfuls, Allison wolfed the food down, and then seemed to relax and enjoy eating. Cory hoped this was a good omen. She kept silent until Allison had finished breakfast.

"Have you heard from Hamid?"

"Yes. He called right after I spoke with you. Said he had a problem with the nanny and had to take care of it at the time he was supposed to phone me."

"Hmm... did he say what kind of a problem?"

"Something about her visa."

Cory calculated the eight hour time difference between Europe and San Francisco and this didn't make sense. Government offices were closed in the evening, but maybe he had special connections with the embassy. It was only an assumption that he was in Europe. He could be in the Middle-East and the time difference would be greater.

"What happened to the nanny you had here?"

"When the children left, she took another job. Since I've agreed to therapy, Hamid wants to come home as soon as possible. He wants to bring the nanny. The kids are very comfortable with her."

"That's great, Allison. Hamid seems to be an intelligent, caring father."

Concentrating on one single patient wasn't Cory's shtick. If Doctor Dick couldn't recommend a therapist for Allison, Cory would call the California Psychological Association to find a local therapist, one who would focus on the psychological problem and wouldn't go off half-cocked on intrigue as Cory had found herself doing.

"Yes. I want to believe Hamid. Truly I do, but somehow... he didn't sound convincing."

"I don't understand."

"I know my husband. We're very close. He'd rather say nothing than lie, but he didn't sound like himself at all. Oh, I don't know, Doctor Cohen. I want us to live as a family again and am scared it won't happen... that something will prevent it. And after my appetite returned, too. See," she said, pointing to her empty bowl.

Cory smiled, understanding the erratic nature of Allison's disease. She hoped this eating disordered patient wouldn't vomit after the session.

"When we want something so much, we're afraid it won't happen, as if it's too good to be true."

"Yes, but I know Hamid. I can read between the lines." She rinsed the utensils and placed them in the dishwasher.

"Why would he lie to you, Allison?"

"That's what I'm worried about."

"When you speak with him today, you can discuss it."

"That's another problem. He won't be able to phone for a few days."

"What reason did he give?" Cory had thought the job here would soon end, but if Allison's hunch was correct...

"That's just it. He said he couldn't explain. Something to do with business."

Perhaps it was Allison's naiveté that had attracted Hamid. Out of her element wrestling with foreign intrigue, Cory felt uneasy.

"I know it seems sudden, but I am improving. Today, when they took my blood at the lab, I wasn't even afraid of the needle." Allison's mood had shifted again.

The walked into the living room and perched on chairs facing each other.

Allison became animated, optimistic, willing to open up.

Cory was ready with questions, mainly about Hamid. She liked the way he cared about his family and wanted to believe he was an honorable man.

"I noticed your crucifix. Are there religious differences between you and Hamid?"

"No. He's not Muslim. His family went to church for social reasons. They're not religious."

Cory paused to think. Mohammed resembled Hamid as much as if they were twins, or at least, brothers, but they had different family names. Mohammed could have had reason to change his. Was she wandering off into far-fetched territory? The mode for many

Middle-Eastern men was bushy dark brows and mustaches. It's easy to fool people with superficial style.

Allison gazed at Cory as if she anticipated gems of wisdom to fall from her lips.

"Despite what's going on, you seem unusually cheerful, Allison." Cory suspected that Allison- the- chameleon enjoyed her moods. Her roller-coaster rides added spice to her otherwise drab daily life.

"Yes, because now I'm hopeful... really want to give up my eating disorder, and truly want to make sure I do. This time I won't quit therapy."

"Admirable, Allison." Yes, she was naive, but not stupid.

"I'm especially happy because Hamid and the kids plan to return—and I hope they will. Oh, Lord, do I ever!"

Cory was planning a few conjoint sessions after his arrival, and then her job with Allison would be over.

At the end of the session, Cory asked for directions to the library. Allison offered her a ride in her limousine since she wasn't due to leave for the bed-and-breakfast for another hour. Cory didn't want to appear ungrateful and accepted. They walked outside together. Allison gave the uniformed driver directions, smiled and waved good-bye.

The chauffeur, with his rod-like posture, fair complexion, steel gray hair and a matching pencil thin mustache, reminded Cory of a German storm trooper.

She wanted to hear his accent, but her attempts at small talk yielded no response. Glancing at the rear view mirror, she noticed his ice blue eyes staring at her, as if committing her to memory. Did he find her an oddity? He gave her the jitters and she was relieved when they reached the library. He opened the car door for her, and drove off without a word or gesture.

Cory entered the building and marched toward the desk. The sign read: *Please turn off your cell phones while in the library.*

She obeyed and had to wait her turn. In this public library, computers seemed to take up more space than books. Cory felt sad for people who couldn't afford to own a laptop and to pay for a link to the internet. Public libraries offered them at least an hour to surf the net and handle their email. If there was no line, they could stay as long as they wanted. It saddened her to see so many people who, judging from their ragged clothing appeared to be homeless. For them, the computer was a crucial link to what was going on in the world, and maybe to their loved ones. After waiting fifteen minutes, it was her turn to use the computer. Finally, she got on the Internet.

She learned that Iran had supplied the Katyusha rockets fired upon Israel. No surprise.

The prestigious *British Intelligence Digest* reported that our administration has withheld vital intelligence data from Israel on Iran's nuclear plans for fear of damaging our relations with Russia, a major Iran supporter. According to the Defense Department, China and Russia have nuclear cooperation agreements with Iran which could accelerate the development of Iran's nuclear weapons. Cory figured North Korea was also involved in this too.

As if this wasn't enough to make her stomach do flip-flops, she read that since the mid-1980s, Iran has an active chemical and biological weapons program.

Cory knew much of the stuff on the Internet could be propaganda, but how to cut the wheat from the chaff? She tried to cross-check references and found it frustrating, but continued to read:

At one time, Secretary of State Madeline Albright, although wary of Iran, stated we did not oppose a trans-Iranian gas pipeline, designed to wind through Iran to deliver gas to Turkey and eventually to Europe. U.S. officials said that the pipeline would not carry Iranian gas, but Iran would collect transit fees.

Cory wondered whether there was American investment in this project.

Rumor had it that corrupt multi-national corporations were in league with democratic governments, serving the interests of those offering financial support. She had learned in her economics class at Brooklyn College that politics was based on economics. There was abundant evidence on that.

The more she read, the more she felt like a naive, impotent human pawn on the chessboard of life. And the more worried she became.

=12=

Cory spent so much time on the Internet that it was dark by the time the librarian kicked her off the computer. Her eyes watered, her head ached and her stomach rumbled.

She taxied to the hotel and ate the Chinese food leftovers, kept fresh in the small refrigerator. The ginger settled her stomach.

It dawned on her that she had forgotten to turn on her cellphone after leaving the library. When she turned it on, there was a message from Ben, but the three hour time difference made her hesitate to return the call. She figured he'd be worried, so at midnight in New York, she phoned a sleepy man.

"Where the hell were you?" he grumbled.

"Hey, wait a minute, Ben. I'm not a child and you're not my parent."

"I'm sorry, Cory. I was worried."

"Oh! You sounded like a disapproving parent."

"Damn it, Cory. It's because I care about you. You're too sensitive."

Yeah, so what else was new? "Good detection." That was their first fight. "I went surfing."

"What?"

"On the Internet, at the library. I wanted to educate myself about oil, and how it helps Iran fund world terrorism."

"Speaking about that, have you heard about the New York arrest? Two young Palestinian punks prepared for a suicide mission—a subway bombing. Stupid fanatics thought they'd go off to paradise in an explosion, but the police acted on a hot tip."

"My God, Ben. You know how many people ride the subway?"

"They probably targeted New York City because it has the largest Jewish population in the United States just like they did in Buenos Aires. You once told me when you were a kid in Brooklyn, you thought the whole world was Jewish."

"True. As a kid, I was surrounded by Jews almost everywhere."

"Listen Cory, one of the men arrested had once lived in Jordan, like you know who."

Mohammed was worthy of watching. What was this clumsy man's mission? Could he be a self-proclaimed spy? A terrorist? Why had he spied on Allison?

Ben continued, "Hamas disclaimed responsibility, but the mayor said he wouldn't believe anything said by a terrorist."

"Thank God they caught these guys. I'm scared they'll continue to blow up places all over the world, Ben."

"You scared? I thought you were tough."

"I am tough. Did I ever tell you how I foiled a murderer?"

"What? No!"

"I woke you up. I'll save the tale for when we're together, which will be—when?"

"Very soon. I need a little more information before I leave. I'll call in the evening and let you know when to expect me. Have you made it to Sausalito yet?"

"Tomorrow. Your client is improving—at least it looks so."

"Can hardly wait to see you, Cory."

"And I, you. Go back to sleep, now. Pleasant dreams."

"They will be, if they're about you. Ciao, Cory.

"Ciao, Ben."

Off to bed Cory went, with a smile on her face which quickly evaporated, because the next thing she knew, she was trudging beside camels in a scorching desert. The stench of dung nauseated her. Hot sand seared her feet and her head ached from the glaring sun. She made for shelter in a tent, but veiled women in formless abayas shunned her and prodded her with a huge stick of dynamite. All the men looked like they were clones with black, bushy eyebrows and mustaches. Each wore a blue and white striped *shmata* fastened with a black cord on his head. They seemed to be cursing in a foreign tongue. Sweat rolled down her back and chest, saturating the clothes that clung to her clammy skin. She felt hot, sticky and suffocating. She tried to cry out, but her parched throat constricted.

13

Cory awoke in the stifling but familiar hotel room. During the night, the heat had gone on full blast. She found herself entangled in bed linens. The sweats she'd worn to bed, now sopping, had earned their name. She peeled them off, pitching them atop the pile of laundry in a brown paper sack and reminded herself to go to the Laundromat today. After guzzling two cups of water, she showered and dressed.

Marching off, paper bag in tow, she located a Laundromat a couple of blocks away adjacent to a cafe. She tossed her stuff into a machine, fed it the necessary coins, sprinkled in detergent, and took herself to breakfast.

This time the scent of maple syrup didn't tempt her, but scrambled eggs and dry wheat toast did. Someone had left a newspaper on the table.

Cory read that Israel wanted to retaliate for Hamas's bombing of the Jerusalem marketplace, by withholding money due the Palestinians and wouldn't permit them to work in Israel until their leader controlled Hamas.

When the server offered a coffee refill, Cory said she'd be right back. She dashed next door to toss the clothes into the dryer. Upon her return, she settled into the chair and sipped the robust brew. The cafe was not busy so she read until it was time to fetch her stuff from the Laundromat.

Back in the hotel room, she removed the laundry from the bag. A tattered slip of lined yellow note paper fell out. What the devil was it doing here? Unfolding it, she read the tiny printed handwriting: *Someone is after you. Be careful.* Perhaps the note was in the bag before she had used it. Perhaps it was meant for the previous occupant of her room. Or had someone pitched it in while she was at breakfast? Was it a prank? If an angel had been watching over her, he or she would have offered more specifics, she thought.

Closing her eyes, she tried to visualize the people she had seen in the Laundromat. Two young women, One young man, and an older woman with a toddler in a stroller. All seemed harmless, concentrating on their business. Someone could have been watching her and slipped it into her bag when she had walked out. But, who? Why?

She dropped the note into her purse and set off for Allison's. On alert, Cory half expected a brick to fall on her head. The air was cool, making it easier to walk briskly, up and down hills. No brick fell and no one followed her.

Allison greeted her with a big smile. She wore a long, blue denim dress and a colorful embroidered vest. Her hair gleamed. Blush on her cheeks and coral colored lipstick gave her a healthy glow.

A cinnamon scent pervaded the house. "Mm . What smells so good, Allison?"

"I've made buns and peach cobblers. I hope you'll have some." She pointed to a serving table behind them. On it was a tray laden with tea and sweets.

"Yes, thank you."

Allison poured the citrus scented tea and offered a bun and a pink paper napkin.

Cory accepted. "Thanks. You look especially well, today."

"I am feeling great. I really do believe I'll lick this thing."

"I like your choice of words, Allison."

"Huh?"

Socially reclusive Allison didn't get humor. "Never mind, I tried to make a joke on your use of the word 'lick,' as it pertains to food."

"Oh, yes! I do see!" she said, clapping her hands. "I wanted you to know that I haven't felt like vomiting since I went to the doctor. And I feel unburdened."

"Great. Your word usage tells me a lot of things, Allison."

"Isn't that what words, do?"

"Sure, but there are underlying meanings in the choice of words. Take for example, *unburdened* that suggests before you'd vomited, you felt burdened, not necessarily from food. Purging relieved the burden."

She cupped her chin in her hand. "Hmm. How interesting. Therapy is truly fascinating."

"It's where you get to unburden, safely."

Allison appeared eager to engage in the process. And so she did. At the close of the session, Cory felt certain she was highly intelligent, but her social isolation had prevented the growth of a sense of humor. The doorbell rang. Cory rose to leave as Allison went to answer the door.

The chauffeur entered carrying a large carton of groceries. She asked him to stock the pantry.

"I plan to ferry over to Sausalito, today. Is it okay if I stop at Mattingly Manor?

"Of course. Tea time is four o'clock and there'll be some goodies for you to take home."

"Thanks." At the door, she waved goodbye.

Pleased with her progress, Cory wanted to skip down the street, but cautioned herself not to jump to conclusions. Propelled by mood swings, Allison could easily regress. They would have to work on her coping mechanisms. If she sank into a deep depression, she might agree to medication. They had made a splendid start, but Cory couldn't stay in San Francisco indefinitely to provide long-term therapy.

With time before the ferry trip, Cory traipsed over to the small cafe where she had last seen Mohammed, to see whether it was still closed.

She glanced at the store window. The shades were drawn and the CLOSED sign was in view. Wondering about what may have happened to the proprietors, she felt jittery. The note in the laundry bag came to mind: *Someone is after you. Be careful.*

She hurried away and hopped on the cable car. She jumped off at the last stop and bought a ferry ticket to Sausalito. With half an hour to mosey around before boarding, she window-shopped and took in the pleasant salt air. Pausing to watch the sea lions sunning themselves on the rocks, she remembered the last time she had seen them was when she had learned of Ingrid's collapse.

Cory called the hospital to ask about her. When the operator said she wasn't in the computer, Cory's heart took a flying leap. "Oh, my God! Is she dead?" she shouted.

"I don't have that information," the operator said.

"May I please speak with administration?"

"One moment."

Cory waited, drumming her fingers until a pleasant voice answered, "Administration. May I help you?"

"Yes, please. This is Doctor Cohen, a friend of Jane Doe, the woman who was brought in comatose Saturday afternoon. I just learned she's not in your computer. What does that mean?"

"Just a moment, please." Cory heard her fingertips click the keyboard. "My records indicate she was discharged today."

"Oh, thank you. Thank you so much."

Assuming she'd return to the hotel for her things, Cory phoned there and left her a message that's she'd be back before seven that evening.

Had she miraculously improved or left against medical advice? What would become of her?

* * *

Boarding the ferry, Cory kept thinking about Ingrid. She wanted to see her; to celebrate her recovery over dinner.

Lulled by the steady hum of the ferry's motor, Cory closed her eyes and imagined a life fraught with foreign intrigue and danger. She dozed off. Just as they reached Sausalito, she awoke feeling groggy. The inside of her mouth felt like sandpaper.

As she disembarked, a teenage boy shoved her aside. She pulled on his arm, but he tugged it away and ran down the gangplank. A pickpocket, she thought and reached into her purse to check for her wallet. She clutched it gratefully, and watched the boy disappear into the crowd.

Straight ahead up a steep hill facing the harbor she saw "Mattingly Manor Bed-and-Breakfast." At a distance the grand old three story white frame structure, royal blue awnings over the windows and front door, looked pleasant and inviting.

It wasn't yet tea time, the hour of her expected arrival, but she was thirsty. Searching for an oasis, she strolled along trendy shop-filled streets and stopped at an old fashioned cafe. Cory ordered mineral water, gulped it down and dipped her hand into her pocket for some change. She pulled out five quarters and a slip of yellow note paper. What the devil was this?

She unfolded it and read the tiny, carefully printed lettering: *Get away from here before it is too late.*

She scanned the faces of the people in the shop for any sign of a suspicious-looking character, but it was impossible to tell. Someone must have paid the hurried teenager to jam the note into her pocket when she had lined up to get off the ferry. She rooted through her purse for the first message and compared the two notes.

The handwriting appeared to be the same. Someone wanted her to keep away from Allison. Well, it was too late. She was already involved and wouldn't turn back. She paid the check and started for Mattingly Manor. She thought of calling Detective Johns, but these notes were warnings, not threats and she doubted he could do much about them.

When she reached the bed and breakfast, the fragrance and blaze of colors of an English style rose garden calmed her. She climbed the staircase to the entrance. White wicker rocking chairs with floral cushions graced the wide porch that wrapped around the house.

Inside the main door, harp music greeted her. She followed the sound past the lobby until she reached a large alcove where about a dozen guests seated in comfortable looking furniture enjoyed tea time.

Cory spotted a vacant chair in the rear of the alcove. The server, a spry white-haired woman bounced toward her and whispered, "May I help you?"

"I'm Cory Cohen. Ms. Mattingly invited me here."

"Oh, yes. We were expecting you. May I bring you something?"

Cory nodded and the white-haired woman went toward a serving station.

As Cory calmed herself in the relaxed ambiance, she thought Mattingly Manor should be a winner among the bed and breakfast crowd.

The server returned and placed a tray on the table beside Cory. Apart from tea, cinnamon buns and peach cobblers, there was a package of goodies with her name on it just as her host had promised. She glanced at the harpist. To her surprise, it was Allison. When Cory had asked her interests, she'd failed to mention the harp. Cory wondered about it. What else had Allison concealed?

* * *

Before she could speak with Allison, she saw her hurrying toward the lobby. Cory chased after her, but she disappeared.

"Gone for the day," the receptionist, a woman with mud-colored eyes that matched her close cropped hair, said when Cory asked for Ms. Mattingly.

Cory was curious why Allison had left in haste and thought it odd that she had offered her a ride in her limousine to the library, but not for her return to San Francisco this afternoon. The receptionist sat at her desk staring at Cory, as if expecting her to make conversation.

"This place is so peaceful and lovely," Cory said.

"Yes, and guests rave about our hearty breakfast and afternoon tea."

"Do you always have live music during tea time?"

"Only when Ms. Mattingly feels up to it." The woman's pale face colored, probably at the realization that she'd revealed too much.

"It was most enjoyable. Do you have a vacant room to show me?"

"No, I'm sorry. We've nothing for the rest of the summer."

"Mind if I look around?"

"Not at all."

Cory strolled through the lobby, puzzling again about what Ben expected her to learn here. Floor-to-ceiling windows offered a spectacular view of the magnificent garden ablaze with purple bougainvillea, and roses of every shade. Beyond, the reflection of the sun shimmered on the water at the wharf.

Cory reached the small guest library. A woman kneeling at the bottom shelf looked up and they exchanged smiles. An older man glanced up from his newspaper and resumed reading. Cory rarely got attention from strange older men.

Next she entered the game room. Two middle-aged bearded men sat in silence opposite each other at a table studying a chess board, while two animated young couples played bridge in a corner of the room. So far, everything appeared normal. She hadn't a clue about what she was supposed to look for.

As she approached the kitchen, she heard a woman shout, "You're fired. Here's your pay for the day. Now get out and don't come back."

The sacked employee, a short, slim, dark haired young man sporting a Fu Manchu style mustache stormed out muttering, "*A tu madre.*"

Uncomfortable at witnessing his humiliation, Cory escaped though the side door to the porch where a young couple cuddled on a swing. Feeling like an interloper, she returned to the lobby.

She was ready to leave, but decided on a quick trip to the powder room. Decorated and scented with a large vase of fresh flowers, the room offered an ample supply of Yardley soap and the softest hand towels. Allison sure knew how to treat guests.

A cuckoo clock struck the time, reminding Cory to hurry in order to catch the next ferry. At the dock she joined a long line of travelers.

Once aboard, she stood at the railing and viewed the San Francisco skyline as they sailed toward the city. A cool bay breeze whipped around her. She raised the collar of her jacket, dug her hands into her pocket where she had fingered the foreboding note. She could hardly wait to see Ben and tell him about the warnings.

After the ferry docked, she headed for the hotel, hoping Ingrid had collected her message.

She checked at the desk, but Ingrid hadn't arrived and there were no messages for Cory.

The salt air had made her hungry, but she was too tired to go out. Although she would have liked to see Ingrid, the idea of crawling into bed with a good book, mellow music, a sandwich and hot tea suited her fine. She didn't want to think about Ingrid, Allison, warning notes, or anything. Except maybe Ben.

She called room service and ordered a turkey sandwich and hot herbal tea to be delivered in thirty minutes.

After a few yoga poses, she flipped on the jazz station and listened to George Shearing's piano rendition of "Lullaby of Birdland." She drummed on the table. Just as the piece finished, the phone rang.

"Ciao, Cory."

"Good to hear your voice, Ben. You okay?"

"Beat from the heat. And you?"

"Fine. Have a lot to tell you. Did you know Allison entertains guests by playing the harp during tea time?"

"No. She never mentioned it," he answered.

"I wonder what else she hasn't told us."

"You're suspicious of her?"

"Not sure. What's going on with you?"

"I'll save it for tomorrow when I see you. I expect to be back at the hotel in time for dinner at eight with my favorite woman."

"Great. Say, Ben. I don't want to worry you, but I've received two warning notes." She read the contents to him.

He whistled. "Listen, Cory, I'll hang up now so you can call Johnny about this." He gave her the number. As soon as they disconnected, she phoned and left a message for his friend.

About fifteen minutes later room service delivered her order just as the phone rang. It was Detective Johns in the lobby, asking to come up. She gave him the room number and pushed the tray aside.

The detective, a heavyset man with a ruddy complexion stood at the door. "Sorry, I've no time to chat. I'm here for the notes, "he said.

"Thanks for coming," she said, handing him the tattered scraps of yellow paper. "I've received these two warning messages. Yesterday morning, I found the first one in my laundry sack. I thought it was a prank or meant for the previous hotel guest, but this afternoon while waiting to get off the ferry on my way to Mattingly Manor, a rude teenager shoved me aside and ran down the gangplank. A few minutes later I discovered the second note in my pocket. I figured he must have stuffed it in there."

The detective scanned the messages before putting them into a plastic bag. "They aren't threats, but as a favor to Ben I'll look into it." He turned on his heel and walked away. Not friendly. In fact, curt, but he had responded quickly.

Cory ate half the sandwich and abandoned the rest, saving her appetite for dessert. She opened the package of goodies from Allison. Honey-glazed raisins and walnuts poked their little heads through the cinnamon-scented bun. She picked up a sticky one and started to munch it, but after few bites she noticed the pastry appeared to be dusted with flour and tasted bitter. She tossed it into the trash and sipped the hot tea.

Cory had difficulty staying awake. It would be good to get up early and hit the pavement for a power walk. She bolted the door, turned off the radio and lamp and drew the covers around her, ready for sleep, but not for long.

Gripped by sharp cramps and waves of nausea, she dashed into the bathroom, not knowing whether to sit on the toilet or on the floor with her head over the bowl. She alternated between both. It felt like there were continuous explosions inside her stomach. She doubled over with stomach pain, grew faint, cold and clammy. Afraid she was dying of food poisoning, she called 9-1-1.

"Please send an ambulance. I've been poisoned! Cory Cohen. Tuscan Hotel. Room 303. Hurry please!" She crawled to the door, unbolted it, and writhing in pain, rolled herself into a ball.

≠14≠

Cory awoke in a hospital bed. Sunlight cast a warm glow on the nurse who stood over her, checking an IV. "How do you feel?" she asked.

"Weak. My stomach feels tender and my throat raw, but the cramps and nausea are gone," she said in a raspy voice.

"That's normal after being purged from ingesting poison."

"I thought I was going to die. How long have I been here?"

"Since last night."

"Last night! Oh, my God! What happened to me?"

"Well, the paramedics took good care of you, Doctor. They're swift and efficient. To keep you out of shock, they started an IV with dextrose and saline, and did a gastric lavage," she said, scanning a chart hanging from the foot of the bed. "They catheterized for a urine specimen and drew a blood sample. You don't remember any of that?"

Cory tried to shake her head, but the room seemed to spin. She noticed Detective Johns seated in the corner. He smiled and came toward her.

"Good morning. How do you feel?"

"I'm not sure. Weak. Dizzy. Should have listened to the warning notes."

"They're up at the fingerprint lab. We'll see if a match is made today."

"Have you been here long?"

"A few minutes."

"You do know that I'm working with Ben?"

The detective nodded and moved his chair to her bedside. "Where did the food in your room come from?" He whipped out a pad and pen.

"The sandwich was delivered from hotel room service. I ate half. Uh—I had some of the cinnamon bun. It felt kind of powdery, not like those I'd eaten earlier." Mentioning the food nauseated her. She knew cinnamon buns would have no place in her future.

"Hmm. Arsenic looks like flour, but the lab will soon let us know. Where did you get the pastry?"

"At a bed and breakfast in Sausalito." She realized Allison would be incriminated. It made no sense. Why would Allison want to poison her? Was that what the warnings were about? Allison seemed naive, not paranoid, and not psychotic. Allison seemed to want her around, if for no other reasons than to assuage her loneliness and to please Hamid.

"Mattingly Manor, huh?" Detective Johns asked.

"Yes. Would you mind calling Allison Mattingly for me? We had an appointment today and obviously—"

"Sure. I have to see her anyway."

"I understand." Cory didn't have the energy to figure out what Ben had wanted her to discover at the inn and why someone wanted her out of the way. Her thoughts became jumbled. "I need to rest— to sleep. I'm sorry, but I can't... " She closed her eyes.

When she awoke, the sun had set, but fluorescent light bathed the room. She had visitors.

At her bedside, stood Allison, sobbing, with Detective Johns at her side. She stared at Cory, then dabbed her eyes with a handkerchief.

"Oh, Doctor Cohen, I am so glad you're okay. When I heard what happened, I was devastated. I baked the pastry myself and wouldn't poison anyone. I can't imagine what happened."

"The lab found traces of arsenic on the bun. We're investigating the staff at Mattingly Manor," Detective Johns said.

"I've had the same employees for several years. I can't understand this. I will cooperate in every way." She fidgeted with her necklace.

"Was anyone else poisoned, Allison?" Cory asked.

"No. Never. I feel truly terrible for you and what you've been through. I heard they pumped your stomach. I'll pay for your medical expenses and then some. If you want to sue me, I'll gladly pay whatever. I'm so ashamed," she sobbed.

"Thank you, Allison. I know you wouldn't deliberately poison me. Detective Johns will find the culprit."

She glanced at him. "I'd like to keep this out of the news, Detective. It could destroy my business."

"We do what we can to prevent a leak to the media, Ms. Mattingly, but it's not always possible," he said.

"As if I don't have enough problems," Allison mumbled.

"I'm curious about something, Allison. Did you notice me at the inn?"

"No. I'm sorry, but I didn't look around. I was distracted—in a hurry to keep a dental appointment. Earlier in the day, I'd instructed the staff to bring you the parcel my chauffeur had placed in the kitchen."

"I was surprised to see you play the harp."

Allison blushed. "That old thing? I'm hardly a professional, you know."

"I enjoyed it."

"Did anything else happen that I should know about?" the detective asked Cory.

She propped up her pillow and leaned back. "Hmm. Maybe this is important. When I was at Mattingly Manor, I overheard a row coming from the kitchen. A woman sacked a young man. It s eemed to me, he was a temporary worker."

Detective Johns took a little pad from his pocket and started scribbling away.

"Can you describe him, please?"

"About early twenties. It's hard to be sure because his Fu-Manchu mustache may have made him look older. He had dark hair and eyes, and he was short and slim. I think he was Puerto Rican."

"Why do think so?" the detective asked.

"He muttered a curse in Spanish. As a former New Yorker, I'm familiar with a Puerto Rican accent. By the way, Ben should be at the hotel at eight. What time is it now?"

"Almost seven-thirty. Don't worry," Detective Johns said. "The hospital will let Ben see you after visiting hours. You should know they considered discharging you today, but Ms. Mattingly thought you should stay until you feel absolutely well enough to leave."

"That's thoughtful, Allison. Actually, I'd like to leave now." Cory pulled her legs to the side of the bed, but when she tried to stand, she became dizzy. "Perhaps you're right. Another night in the hospital won't kill me."

* * *

Sometime after the detective and Allison had gone, Cory became hungry. The tray by her bedside, ignored during dinner, suddenly looked inviting. The pot of tea was cool to the touch and the apple juice, room temperature, but the cubes of glimmering red Jell-O were as appealing as an ice cream sundae on a hot day. Cory snatched a spoonful and was about to swallow it when her throat closed up. She recognized the symptom: acute stress disorder, a condition that often follows a shock such as hers in which the sufferer fears a recurrence of the episode.

If the person who had tried to poison her knew she was alive and knew where she was, he or she could do it, again! Surely Detective Johns realized that, yet she saw no sign of any protection. Angry and frightened, she wanted to escape, but when she tried to get out of bed, the room spun. "I must get better. I must leave," she told herself.

She rang for the nurse and within minutes a dark haired, petite young woman with a dimpled smile appeared.

"May I help you?" she asked.

"Yes. Would you please remove the IV, and may I have bottled water or a can of apple juice, please?"

"We were instructed to keep the IV in until you ate and drank on your own. How about a fresh cup of juice?"

"Yesterday, I was poisoned and now I'm afraid to drink anything from an opened bottle."

"Oh, I understand. I'll get you a can from the machine." She started to leave.

"No thanks. I don't have any money here."

The thoughtful nurse shrugged, left the room and in a few minutes returned holding a bottle of Gatorade. Making a show of tearing off the plastic wrap, she unscrewed the bottle and handed it to Cory. With a flourish, she presented a cellophane wrapped straw.

Cory smiled in gratitude. The nurse removed the IV and left her alone.

With nothing to do, she sipped and ruminated about who could have poisoned her and why she was the target.

Perhaps someone wanted to keep her away from Allison to stop her from learning information that could hurt a cause, as yet unknown to her. This person had tailed her without raising suspicion. If Ben couldn't get here tonight, she had to rely on herself.

She knew she was vulnerable and wouldn't be safe at the hotel, but she needed her identification, money and credit cards. Too weak and dizzy to get out of bed, she lay blanketed by helplessness. Now, she really knew how Ingrid had felt fleeing from her abusive husband—trapped in dread. Cory's eyes welled with tears and her fists were tightly balled. Not knowing anyone to ask to cart her from the hotel, she flashed on the helpful nurse. She would offer payment and was about to ring for her when Ben dashed into the room. "Wow! Am I glad to see you!" she sighed.

"Cory! I'm so sorry." He sat on the bed, leaning over her for a hug. "It's my fault for getting you into this mess." He ran his fingers through her hair, comforting her.

"You couldn't know."

"How do you feel?"

"One thousand percent better since you showed up."

"Johnny left me a message. I'd have come earlier, but I had to gather up our stuff at the hotel and check out."

She noticed he'd placed all her stuff on the chair. "Thank God! I was afraid to go back there, Ben. I'm surprised your so-called friend didn't have someone watch over me here."

"Huh? An officer's been sitting outside your room since they brought you in, Cory."

"I wish he'd told me. I was scared. I couldn't eat, and now I'm hungry."

"Good sign. There's a canteen in the waiting room. I'll get something light."

"Thanks."

"Be right back," he said, rushing out.

A few minutes later he returned with a container of tea in one hand, juice in the other, and a bag of pretzels clutched in his teeth.

"Manna from Heaven," she said after her first bite. "I'd like to leave here as soon as possible, but where can we go?"

"Johnny offered us his place in Santa Cruz, not too far from here. We can use a little holiday for a few days. It's safer than returning to San Diego now."

"But Allison needs me."

"She can have phone sessions. I'll call her now—tell her I'm back and that you'll call the inn on Monday at one-thirty."

"This reminds me. Why did you want me to investigate Mattingly Manor? Nothing struck me as suspicious."

"I wanted your take on it. If something was odd, you'd know."

"Thanks for the compliment, Ben, but you're the real detective."

"Don't underestimate yourself, Cory. Anyway, I'm not perfect."

She squeezed his hand. "To me, you're as close to it as possible."

"And I'd like to get as close to you as possible." He smiled. "Hopefully, you'll be discharged tomorrow. Listen, I'll ask Johnny to send the officer away and have a cot rolled in for me." He kissed her forehead and whispered, "I'd prefer crawling into bed with you."

Cory fell asleep grinning.

꞊15꞊

Awakened by squeaking wheels from the cart in the hallway outside her room, she looked around and saw Ben, fully clothed, sleeping on a cot, his jacket rolled under his head. Cory felt a mixture of guilt for allowing him to stay, and gratitude that he had. She realized he felt responsible and wanted to watch over her, but she knew it wasn't just out of obligation. He genuinely cared, a new and precious thing for her to absorb from a man. With pleasure, she studied his face, his thick dark hair, his large, sturdy form. A strong, but gentle guy. A friend.

The lab tech came into the room to draw blood. Ignoring the sleeping man, he raised his voice and affected a Rumanian accent: "Count Dracula is here to bite you." Cory laughed as he handed her a palm sized rubber ball to squeeze. "Glad you have a sense of humor, Doctor Cohen." Completing his mission, he smiled and wheeled his cart out.

Ben stirred, opened his eyes, rolled off the cot and stretched. "How do you feel, Cory?"

"If the room doesn't whirl when I get off the bed, I'm fine."

"I'm going to clean up," he said, escaping into the restroom.

A few minutes later the nurse arrived and took Cory's vital signs. "Everything's fine. Feeling better?"

"Let's see." Cory pulled her legs over the edge of the bed and stood. She still felt weak, but the dizziness was gone. "Yes, thank you. Will I be able to leave soon?"

"Probably after the doctor examines you. He's on his rounds now."

Ben stepped out clean shaven, sporting jeans and a short-sleeved shirt.

Cory hurried through her morning ritual, making sure to swish a pleasant mint mouth wash. When she rummaged through her carry-on for something to wear, she noticed that the paper on which she had written notes about Mohammed was opened flat. She remembered having folded it in quarters before stashing it away. Hurriedly, she slipped into sweatpants and a baggy T shirt that read, "DON'T MESS WITH ME." She opened the bathroom door and waved the paper. "Ben, I'm positive I'd folded this. Did you happen to read it when you packed my stuff?"

"No." He took the paper from her. "I was in a rush to get here and just pitched all your stuff into your bag. Are you absolutely certain you folded it?" he asked, studying her writing.

"Yes, it's a habit. Someone must have searched my room."

"Johnny's investigating the hotel staff in connection with the poisoning. I'll ask him to check this for prints." Ben picked up the phone and paged Detective Johns. "We'll have to keep a low profile, Cory."

The doctor arrived, examined Cory, reviewed her chart, asked a few questions and pronounced her well enough for discharge. He advised her to eat lightly for a day or so—as if she could imagine otherwise.

They started out the door when Ben received a call from Detective Johns.

"He said a uniformed officer was on his way here to collect the notes."

"Good. "she said, nodding her head.

Ben paced the corridor like an expectant father as Cory rested.

Ten minutes later, the officer arrived and stored the paper in a plastic envelope.

Ben's hand on Cory's elbow steadied her as they walked slowly down the hall. The nurse ran after her rolling a wheelchair. "Wait! Hospital policy. Patients must be wheeled to the door."

The nurse pushed the chair while Ben ran to get the car.

As they headed out of San Francisco, Cory stared out the rear window.

"Cory, stop worrying. We aren't being followed. Think about something else. Something pleasant. Think about us.

"I do. A lot, but I've just left a hospital where I felt vulnerable and dependent and was reminded of Ingrid. Yesterday, she was discharged from the same place. Do you know if she returned to the hotel or left a note for me?"

"You had no messages and there was no sign of her."

"Odd, huh?"

"Yes. Well, she survived and that's that, Cory."

"I'll always wonder what became of her."

"Uh-huh," he said, adjusting the rear view mirror.

"It's strange, Ben, but I hadn't noticed anyone following me."

"A professional."

"What? You mean I'm not a professional because I didn't realize it?"

He patted her knee. "No. The tail was professional."

"I see. I keep reviewing the sequence of events. I remember the server gave me the package of Allison's baked goods during tea time. Who could've tampered with it? The voyage from Allison's kitchen to my hands needs to be traced."

"Johnny's job. He's checking her staff."

"I hope that includes those who work at her house too."

"Johnny will do what needs doing, sweetheart."

They stopped for a red light and Ben shifted into park, leaned over and kissed her. "Yearned for this," he said.

Too quickly, the traffic signal changed to green and off they went onto a narrow highway that hugged the breathtaking magnificent coast.

"The scenic view's worth the slow drive. We'll make a pit stop around Half Moon Bay and grab some grub," Ben said.

With Ben beside Cory, she felt secure. She adjusted the seat to recline and dozed off.

"Damn!" Ben cursed, waking her up.

"What's wrong?"

"Engine is smoking. The damn car is sputtering. It's dying on us." Ben tried in vain to pull the car off the highway.

Afraid of someone rear-ending them, Cory glued her eyes to the rear window. Her pulse raced. "Should we wait on the shoulder?"

Before Ben could answer, a car screeched behind them and whipped around to the side of the road. The driver stepped out and offered assistance. Together the two men pushed the Buick on to the shoulder. After thanking him, Ben called the auto rental agency for a replacement. They said they'd get there within half an hour. A tow would be sent for the disabled vehicle and a blue Infiniti to pick them up. Still woozy, Cory leaned against the car while they waited.

"Maybe I'm getting paranoid, but after what happened to me, I'm wondering if someone tampered with the Buick."

"Listen, Cory. When I'm on a case I'm especially careful to check out my vehicle. It's a good thing this didn't happen on a busy freeway."

"What could be wrong with the car?"

"Like people, cars are unpredictable."

"Yes, but what do you think happened?"

"Okay, Cory. Someone could've followed me to the hospital and put a grinding compound into the air cleaner. I wouldn't have noticed until the engine died out."

The sun poked through the clouds, brightening the sky. Cory reached into her purse for her sunglasses. "So even if you check out the car, there are things you could miss?"

"Sure. I check obvious things, such as the tires, the brakes, and any devices that could be planted to set off explosives."

This was chilling. Cory had to change the subject. "What did you learn in D.C., Ben?"

"Unfortunately, not too much. Hamid is a law-abiding naturalized citizen. Pays income taxes, is credit worthy. He's clean as a whistle. Last 1090 came from Pru-petrol big bucks. My guess is if he's working now, it's for Pru-petrol. I doubt he'd take the kids to the Middle East. He's probably in Paris or London where Pru-petrol has offices."

Cory grew tired leaning against the car and shifted position. "Does that mean you'll travel abroad, if Hamid doesn't return the kids?"

"What makes you think he won't?"

"I don't know. Just a hunch, Ben."

"You may be right. If he's contracted on a project for a multinational oil company, he may not be able to leave right away."

"Hmm. Multinational? I'd like to know which countries are involved."

"Probably at least one that supports terrorism through oil revenue."

Afraid of danger from the oncoming traffic, Cory scanned the road for the blue Infiniti.

"His last contract was for six months. And because his work was proprietary, he wasn't able to travel abroad. I guess the company is afraid someone will steal trade secrets from him."

Cory remained standing at the roadside with her hands on her hips. "If they plan to reconcile, why doesn't he tell Allison where they are so she can go get them?"

"One reason. She's afraid of flying."

"Ah-hah! That's why Hamid was eager to get a visa for the nanny so she would do it."

Ben smiled. "That would be nice, but it's a supposition, Cory."

"After they arrive, our job's done, yes?"

"Unless that Mohammed guy is out to get her. And now that you're helping Allison with her problem—"

"I can't stay here indefinitely, Ben. I'll make provisions for her care."

He glanced at a blue car slowing toward us. "Wait! Here it comes." "Let's make sure we grab all our gear."

The driver jumped out. He was a young man clad in a green plaid flannel shirt over a gray T-shirt and dirty jeans. "Executive Rental," he stuttered and opened the rear passenger door and trunk. Ben pitched their stuff into the trunk and hopped in back. Cory searched the Buick for leftover items and withdrew a map that had fallen to the floor. "We've got everything," She slung her purse over her shoulder and started to step in the back.

"No, here." The driver patted the seat beside him. "The rear seat-belt is broken."

Cory thought it odd, but stepped in. The driver whisked them away.

Ben unfolded the map and studied it. "You're going away from Half Moon Bay. What route are you taking?" he asked the driver, but the man didn't answer.

⸗16⸗

"I asked about the route? Didn't you hear me?"

The driver, a short, stocky young man in his twenties with red hair and freckles, shrugged.

"Maybe he's hard of hearing or doesn't understand English very well, Ben?"

"Stop! *Termina! Halte! Pausa!*" Ben shouted, but the driver hit the gas pedal and they sped down the road. "Damn! My phone is in the trunk," Ben whispered in her ear.

Cory prayed for a Highway Patrol car to catch up with them, but after several miles, the Infiniti slowed and turned off at an unpaved intersection amidst patches of weeds. The car bounced along the bumpy terrain, making Cory queasy. "Stop! Let me out! I'm going to throw up!" She gagged and covered her mouth.

"Aw, shit!" The driver growled, slowing to a stop. He pulled a small pistol from the waistband of his jeans and poked Cory with it. "Go!" he shouted pointing in the direction of a scrawny tree a few yards away. "And you," he said to Ben. "You don't try nothin' or she gets wasted!" He fiddled with the controls on the door panel, hopped out and slammed the door.

Cory glanced back at Ben who was trying in vain to lift the door latch. It probably had a child-proof lock that wouldn't open when the engine was off. Hit by a paroxysm of panic, Cory covered her mouth with her hand and tottered toward the tree. The man followed her. Kneeling, she feigned the dry heaves. Her mind raced as she garnered strength, born from fear and need. He approached her, his hand holding the gun relaxed at his side, "You done?"

Cory's muscles tensed. She whirled around, raising her leg. "KIAI!" She shouted, swiftly kicking the gun from his hand.

Frozen, he stared at her then dropped on all fours to retrieve the fallen weapon, but Cory stamped her foot on his hand and shoved him to the ground. His face hit the dirt with a thud. Blood ran from his nose as he lay stunned. Cory grabbed his keys and gun and raced toward the Infiniti.

Stumbling, the red-haired man tried to chase her, but she reached the car before he could catch her. She slid the key into the door, slammed it shut, and stepped on the gas pedal.

"Stop. Give me the gun. I'm going after him," Ben shouted, leaping over the seat to open the front door.

Her heart raced as she watched him sprint into the woods in pursuit of the red-haired goon.

She prayed, listened for gunshots, but heard none.

She waited. It seemed like forever. Finally Ben returned alone.

"*Sonofabitch*! I couldn't find him in the dense woods. Thank God, you're okay, Cory. Nice job you did."

"I took karate for over twenty years. Haven't been practicing, but when I need it—wham!"

"A black belt, huh?"

She nodded.

"What else are you going to spring?"

"Makes it interesting. You have the map. Where to?"

"Get on the main road and exit at the first sign of life."

Cory slowed the car to fasten the seat belt and they bounced along the path, dust clouding the windshield. Shuddering, she glanced at the revolver. "It looks like a toy."

"Don't be deceived by appearances. Who'd think you're so tough?"

"Time to 'fess up, Ben. Weapons scare the hell out of me. Do you have one?"

Ben carefully placed the gun in the glove compartment. "No. Most PIs in California don't. Either this guy is real stupid or knows I don't carry. I'd have busted the window and his rump."

Cory pulled into the main road and drove in the direction they had been going before they had exited. She glanced at the gas gauge, which registered empty, and headed for the next intersection, but the desolate terrain seemed to continue forever. Afraid to run out of fuel before reaching civilization, she nosed the car on to the shoulder and parked.

Ben hopped out and grabbed his phone from his briefcase in the trunk. He punched a digit connecting him to the California Highway Patrol and related the incident while struggling to pinpoint their location on the map—somewhere off 92 near Crystal Springs. Finally the CHP's sophisticated equipment announced they had spotted them: "The call's been relayed to the Sheriff and they're on their way. They'll get us out of here and look for the guy who hijacked us."

"I screwed up, Ben. I should have gotten his ID while he was down."

"Listen, Cory. There wasn't time. You had to make a run for it. You took a big chance when you kicked him. For God's sake, he could have shot you. I was the one who screwed up. I should have had the phone in my pocket. Never again!"

"But I—"

"Quit thinking about it. You were terrific, you hear?"

Cory paused, trying to figure out how they had gotten into this predicament. "The scenario—maybe this is how it went. Whoever's behind this has been stalking us from the beginning. They rigged the Buick to capture us, expecting you to call from a cellphone to the car rental place. The call was intercepted and the Infiniti sent to help was waylaid by the redhead."

"Okay, Detective Cohen. Why?"

"To see how much we know about Hamid and Allison and to stop our investigation. My God! If they're terrorists, they'd have killed us."

"Sweetheart, I'm impressed." He patted her thigh. It felt comforting. The adrenaline began to dissipate and in its place she felt a moment of calm. She savored the joy their partnership held—mutual respect, adoration, or something close to love.

"Johnny sent the warning notes to the fingerprint unit connected to the FBI computer. If the prints are on file, then bingo, we'll know the identity of your angel."

"Which may lead to who in hell is after us!" She shivered, feeling like a fresh caught fish tossed into an ice barrel.

"Cory, you're shaking. Here, let me warm you." Ben wrapped his strong arms around her. "Sorry you hooked up with me?"

"Despite this danger, absolutely not." She admitted to herself there was a part of her that actually loved the thrill, the intrigue—an unresolved element in her personality. Perhaps it added to the attraction she had felt for Ben right from the start.

"Cory, *shaina n'shuma*," Grandma's voice came to her as it did whenever it was needed. "Don't fumble in darkness. Keep safe so you can help others."

But the treacherous dark lured, challenging her to shine light on the hidden. It propelled her toward detection.

Now, sitting safely beside Ben, she thought Grandma would be happy if she knew of his goodness. She wished she could share her joy with the woman who was more than her grandma—she was a role model of everything good in human beings. She'd nurtured Cory with love and affection that more than made up for the loss of her mother—her father's wife who'd abandoned them a few months after Cory's birth.

The woman was a self-centered person ill-equipped to handle marriage and a child in a culture different from her own. Cory knew little about her, only that she, like Cory's father, was a professional violinist who met Cory's father when they played in a symphony orchestra together touring Europe. When she became pregnant, they came to New York to settle, but she found it stifling and unbearable. A few months after Cory was born, she returned to Japan and wasn't seen or heard from again.

You're so quiet. Are you okay?" Ben asked.

"Much better than expected under the circumstances."

Ben kissed her forehead, just as Grandma had done during Cory's childhood to gauge her temperature.

The windows had fogged up. Cory poked around the control panel until she disconnected the childproof locks and rolled down the windows. Ben gave her a sideways glance. "Okay. So I'm technically challenged. Mechanically dysfunctional," she said.

He chuckled. "Finally, a flaw!"

"More than one. I love music, but can't carry a tune."

"Maybe I can help. I was in my high school choir."

"I'm beyond tonal redemption, but I enjoyed listening to you sing. Maybe the holes in my head fit the bumps in yours."

"And how, sweetheart."

It seemed they both knew their chatter would alleviate their tension. They babbled on until two black and whites bearing the Sheriff insignia pulled behind them and three deputies and a dog jumped out.

Cory and Ben stepped out of the Infiniti and Ben presented his identification. "The gun's in the glove compartment. Doctor Cohen collected it, so you'll find both our prints on it."

"How did you do that, ma'am?" the officer asked while she handed him her driver license.

"Karate."

"Yeah?" He stared at her, then copied her ID and smiled as he returned it.

His partner climbed into the blue car, tossed the gun into a plastic bag and jumped out. "The vehicle will be dusted for prints before returning it to the owner. A unit's on the way. Now if you'll come with us, you can show us where the altercation took place. The perp couldn't have gone far by foot. The dog will sniff him out while you're taken to the station for a statement. You can wait for us and get transportation from there."

Ben hauled their stuff into the Sheriff's vehicle. The two deputies were congenial and appeared willing to help. Cory guessed this incident was the most excitement they'd had in a long time in this remote area.

Cory started to give directions, but her geographical dyslexia became evident and Ben took over. He remembered twists and turns she had forgotten. *Yes, the holes in my head fit the bumps in his,* Cory thought.

In a short time they arrived at the second crime scene. The first, where they were captured, would yield no evidence. The other black and white vehicle nosed beside them and the deputy and his dog jumped out.

Cory pointed to the tree. "That's where I kicked the gun away from him. Bloodied his nose—so there should be stains near the tree. And here's his description: red-haired, freckled-faced, young— maybe twenties. He wore a loose green plaid shirt over a gray T-shirt and dirty jeans."

The deputies took off in pursuit while they were driven to the Sheriff's station.

From watching police dramas on TV and a visit to the San Diego station, Cory found the drab conference room familiar but uncomfortable. Ben seemed at home, shooting the breeze with the detectives. She noticed he avoided mentioning his former work. He was just one of the regular guys working on a case that had resulted in their capture by a guy figured as a two-bit thug hired for a mission to frighten them from continuing their efforts. The officers would need information to trace the redhead to his employer, but there was little to provide. Either they seemed to accept that they were out of their league, or didn't want the work.

Seated on a brown vinyl chair adorned with a patch of black electric tape, Cory scrutinized the sole wall decoration—a poster featuring photos of the FBI's Ten Most Wanted. She was relieved that not one of the faces appeared familiar.

A deputy brought Styrofoam cups of hot tea. "Try to relax," he said. "We'll hear as soon as he's apprehended. Shouldn't be long."

"Thanks," Cory said, reaching for the cup as though it held curative powers.

"The boys in the lab are working on the prints left on the weapon. They'll have their hands full with the Infiniti. Unless it was just washed before driven to you, there could be prints from gas station attendants, mechanics, car-washers and customers."

An officer asked Ben to wait outside the conference room while he instructed Cory to dictate and sign a statement describing the incident. When she finished, she and Ben changed positions.

The deed done, the detective opened the door for Cory to re-enter. Ben was speaking on the phone to someone at Executive Auto Rental.

When his call ended, his face darkened. "Bad news. They refused my patronage. I'm a designated risk. Can't blame them, but it creates a problem."

"How about another company?" Cory suggested.

"Uh-uh. No doubt I'm blacklisted."

"Okay, partner. I'll rent. You navigate."

The deputy glanced at his watch. "I'll be off duty soon. There's a car rental agency on my way home. I can drop you there."

"Thanks. If the perp isn't found by the time you check out, we should leave." Ben took out one of his cards, scrawled Johnny's address and phone number in Santa Cruz and handed it to the officer. "This is where we'll be for awhile. My partner here was discharged from the hospital today and I don't want to add to her stress."

About fifteen minutes later, the desk phone rang and the officer answered it. "I see. Okay. Thanks." He hung up. "They combed the area for the guy, but he's gone. Judging from freshly made tire marks, he was probably picked up by a car near where he pulled off the road. We'll let you know any developments."

They left the station with the off-duty officer. Within twenty minutes Cory had rented a brand new silver Camry with a great sound system. The jazz station came through clearly as they headed for Santa Cruz, Ben singing the lyrics to "Someone To Watch Over Me."

≈17≈

"It's only eighty miles south from San Francisco to Johnny's, but the way we've been deterred it seems forever. If you're tired, we can spend the night at a bed and breakfast on the way." Ben said.

"Are you kidding?"

"Bad joke. I'm sorry. We'll be there before dark. "

They tried to relax looking at the greenhouses and farmlands along the way.

"You'll like where we're going. It's real funky. A university town in a rustic setting. Unlike where we went to school. Great places to hike. I'll whip up some grub in Johnny's dynamite kitchen. You'll like the chow in the veggie cafes, too." Ben seemed to enjoy talking about his pal's hide-away—a place to unwind. To find much needed peace.

"Sounds like paradise," Cory said.

He nodded. "We'll be getting off this road soon."

They drove south down the coast, past sea cliffs, where northern California is at her best. Her purple majestic Santa Cruz Mountains dressed a clear blue sky. Approaching the summit, Cory slowed to take in the scenic beauty.

Thirty minutes later they approached a cut-off.

"Turn here and catch a view of the redwood trees. One day, we'll take a trip to see the giant redwoods."

Cory liked the way he planned a future together.

When they pulled into town, Ben pointed to a vegetarian restaurant decorated with philosophical graffiti. Cory zipped the car into a nearby parking space.

They held hands walking through the open doorway of the sandalwood-scented cafe. Student types buzzed about. Most of the men wore an abundance of earrings and creative hair-dos—spiked, dyed and moussed. The women appeared to be from a distant place or time—wannabes from India or the sixties, embroidered velvet vests over long flowing soft dresses.

To calm her abused stomach, Cory inquired about the mildest dish on the menu. The server, doubling as chef, offered to cook vegetables and puree them into an unseasoned broth. Cory thanked her.

As the server-chef turned, her jewel studded nostril glimmered in the lamplight.

A few minutes later, the accommodating young woman placed freshly baked sourdough bread on the table, its aromatic steam raising their appetites. "You're right, Ben. This place sure is wonderful," Cory said loud enough for the server-chef to hear.

After they left the cafe, Cory felt rejuvenated and fully recovered. While Ben shopped at the market, she strolled the main street, stopping at a used bookstore to examine the obscure titles in the windows, and announcements of events posted on the door. She would have enjoyed spending her graduate school years amidst the quiet natural beauty conducive to study, instead of the incessant noise on the concrete Isle of Manhattan.

In a short while, Ben trudged from the shop lugging two large brown bags filled to the brim. "Don't worry. I got the right stuff for you." He set the packages in the trunk. "Straight ahead. Make two lefts and we're there."

Cory rolled the Camry into the gravel driveway tucked in a wooded area and parked. Their footsteps echoed as they traipsed to the front door, luggage and groceries in tow. Leaves rustled on the trees and somewhere in the distance, a crow cawed.

Ben unlocked the door to Johnny's meticulously clean and tidy cottage. A massive stone fireplace occupied one wall of the living room, and a barrel of firewood stood at its side.

"Time to recharge my phone," he said. Off he went in search of an electrical outlet.

At one end of a huge tan leather couch sat a squat bookcase whose top doubled as an end table. Cory fingered the handsome red leather-bound volumes of classic mysteries by Poe, Conan Doyle, Gardner, and Chandler. "Good bed companions," she remarked as Ben returned.

"I've got a better one," he said, smiling.

"Me too."

It was late summer, but cool and damp in the house. Ben built a fire. Cuddling on the couch, they watched the flames dance, and listened to the crackling wood. Cory felt as if they had shared a long history instead of a memorable trauma. Here they were, safe and alone with time to enjoy each other. She felt comforted, resting her head on his shoulder.

He ran his fingers through her hair and drew his finger along the contour of her jaw. "I've grown accustomed to your face," he sang, like a lullaby, his voice-- rich, warm.

When the fire died, they went into the bedroom where there was a huge shiny, spotless Jacuzzi. Ben scrubbed it before turning the jets on. They slipped off their clothes off and washed each other. Touched by their intimacy, Cory's eyes welled. Ben kissed her tears away.

⸗18⸗

The weekend at Johnny's proved to be a fantastic treat. Ben and Cory's relationship grew deeper and she knew it wasn't just a physical attraction. She loved everything about him, his humor, and his tenderness. Well, almost everything. Cory was ambivalent about his choice of profession. It was exciting but dangerous. She had sufficient experience with danger and did not relish exposing herself to it. Electronic sleuthing was one thing, but cavorting with danger was another. Cory understood the allure, but she had no appetite for it as a steady diet. Probing mysteries of the psyche was much safer.

After having her life threatened in the role of detective, she considered returning to San Diego, but Grandma had taught her not to be a quitter. And she didn't want to leave Ben, especially not in the middle of this murky case. She was also caught up in the intrigue.

They sat at the dining table, sipping coffee and munching bagels, deciding their next move.

"After being tailed and nearly murdered in San Francisco, I'm not eager to go anywhere near Allison. Since I promised, I'll call today and we'll plan her phone sessions."

"You can make those calls from anywhere, Cory. Perhaps you should go home now."

"No. I prefer being with you and finishing my job."

"Listen, sweetheart, I care about you, more than I dreamed possible, and I don't want you harmed."

"Then let's decide how to arrange security and still do the job."

"Avoid going near her house or the bed and breakfast," he said, pouring more coffee into their cups.

Just then, his phone rang and Ben picked it up.

"Yes. We're okay. Thanks. So that's that, huh? Thanks for letting me know. 'Bye."

"What was that about, Ben?"

"That was the Sheriff. Fingerprint techs found no match on the computer search. Our thug is a small-time punk who was lucky and hasn't been caught yet."

"This makes a case for requiring fingerprints on all licenses, Ben. I had to be fingerprinted for my first psychology license. I think it's a good idea."

He nodded agreement. And I thought you were a tree hugging liberal."

"I hold many liberal views, but I'm all for keeping safe, especially after this escapade," Cory said, stacking the brunch dishes. She carried them to the kitchen and began to rinse and pop them into the dishwasher when she overheard Ben speaking on the phone to Johnny. She wiped her hands on a paper towel and dashed toward the phone just as he hung up.

"Sorry, sweetheart. No usable prints on your note paper. Johnny's interviewing more people. Many of the hotel staff aren't on duty. He's e-mailing me their data and I'll run background checks on them and Allison's part-time household staff. So far, everyone at the inn seems clean."

"But how private is the computer?"

"Johnny's a whiz with technical stuff. He devised a foolproof encryption program. We're secure."

"I'm sorry, I didn't mean to imply—"

"It's okay, sweetheart. Shows you're careful."

"It appears your friend is as scrupulous about his job, as he is about his house."

"His passion for order can be annoying." He wiped the table, finding a crumb Cory had missed.

She wondered about his close relationship with Johnny, who seemed formal and stiff, so unlike Ben. "You must be real close for him to let you stay here."

"We've been through a lot together. I guess he appreciates me for having saved his ass."

"How?" *Don't be a yenta,* she heard Grandma's caution in her head.

He paused. She figured he was stalling to avoid revealing a confidence.

"In the line of duty. No time to talk about it now. I've got to get this work out of the way." He marched down the hall to Johnny's office, which was a marvel of neatly arranged papers and books.

Cory sank into the leather sofa and read Sherlock Holmes, feeling much like his side-kick, Doctor Watson. There she stayed until it was time to phone Allison.

Allison picked up at the first ring. "Thank God you've called." Her tremulous voice sounded like she'd been crying, or was bulimic. "The children—they've been kidnapped!"

"Oh no! How?"

"They were grabbed away from the nanny in the park. A cyclist ran her down. During the commotion someone snatched the kids."

"And the cyclist?"

"Disappeared!"

"The police?"

"Scotland Yard is on it, now. I tried calling Ben's mobile, but it didn't ring."

"We were out of range. Just a minute, I'll get him." Cory ran into the office and relayed the news.

Ben took her phone. "I'll contact the Yard. Give me details." He put her on speaker.

Cory listened to the rest of their conversation. Allison had little information. She didn't know the names of the nanny or the police investigator. At least she now had Hamid's London address and phone number.

"Allison, I'm confident that the children will be found," Cory said, trying to sound convincing.

The young mother was inconsolable. Her words could barely be heard through her sobs.

"Alive—ransom—all I have. Hamid promised we'd get them back. Why did they pick our kids? Oh my Lord, why?"

"I'll leave for London as soon as possible and meet with Scotland Yard. We'll do everything possible to get them back," Ben said. "Do you want to come, Allison?"

"I... I'm scared to... and I don't have a passport."

"We'll take care of it. Under these circumstances, I'm sure the State Department can push it through."

"I'm so afraid. Please, Doctor Cohen. I need you. Can you come too?" she pleaded.

Cory glanced at Ben. He shrugged his shoulders and whispered, "You decide."

"Yes, Allison."

"Do you have your official birth certificate handy?" he asked.

"No. I'll look for it, Allison said. "If it doesn't turn up, I'll go to the Bureau of Records, tomorrow." Now that she had a plan, she'd begun to regroup.

"Okay. Let's meet at one thirty at—just a moment, I'll look it up." He clicked a few keys on the computer. "Here it is. The San Francisco Regional Passport office. Ninety-Five Hawthorn Street. Bring your birth certificate, two passport photos and about one-hundred dollars in cash. Call me if anything turns up, or page me. Try here first." He gave her Johnny's number.

"I know this is hard on you, Allison. You're not alone. We'll help," Cory added. "I'll get in touch with you in the morning." She clicked off.

"This can take a big chunk of your time, Cory. Are you sure you can do it?"

"I'll fly to San Diego, take care of business, get my passport and be ready to leave with you." Cory figured they'd be in London by the end of the week. She hoped they weren't too late.

⸗19⸗

The next day, Tuesday, Ben drove slowly through the fog to San Francisco airport for Cory's flight to San Diego. She called Allison who was doing her best to keep herself together. She'd found her birth certificate and would meet Ben on schedule. Neither she nor Hamid had heard from the kidnappers. She was afraid to fly, but knew she had to be there with Hamid when the children were found. At least she had hope that they would be reunited.

Cory's trip home was uneventful. No odd seatmates needed her attention. She wondered where Ingrid was and how was she getting along.

She arrived at Lindbergh Field and hailed a cab. In light traffic, they breezed along Harbor Drive towards the freeway. Modern buildings glistened in the sunlight and sailboats decorated the bay. San Diego offered her a special brand of security and serenity. She took a deep breath and relaxed as they drove up Interstate 5 passing Mission Bay where picnickers, joggers and bike riders were enjoying the usual mild weather. In twenty minutes, they approached Del Mar. Multi-colored hot-air balloons adorned the clear blue sky.

Her empty, quiet house seemed strange to her, as usual whenever she had been away for a few days. She dumped the contents of her carry-on into the washing machine, sprinkled detergent and turned it on. She recalled the note she came upon in the laundry bag in San Francisco and wondered again who'd written it. She watered her thirsty plants and set them outside for the gardener.

The little red light on her office phone blinked five messages. She hit the replay button. Her children Rachel and Noah had called on the same day. This happened often. Was it serendipity or had they planned to do it together? She was pleased that her adult children were close. She remembered when they were little kids, Noah had often teased Rachel. She understood this behavior was typical with opposite sex siblings.

Although they knew she was away, they knew she'd love hearing what they were up to and would chuckle at their humorous antics. They were bright spots in her life. The rest of the calls were hang-ups.

She left voice messages on her children's phones telling them she was leaving for London on a business trip for a few weeks and would contact them from there.

Cory phoned Betty who had covered her absence. Betty said there were no referrals and no emergencies, but there had been a strange call on Friday. "I wasn't sure if it was woman or a man. It seemed to come from a phone booth on a noisy street—something about warning for you to stay clear of Emma."

"Emma? Are you sure?"

"No. I'm not. Could have been Em."

"Could it have been A M?"

"Maybe."

"Did you get the caller's name?"

"No time. The person thought I was you, Cory. Sounded disappointed that I wasn't. I said your service had patched your call here and I was covering for you. Will you tell me what's going on?"

Cory filled Betty in on her adventures and travel plans. After a few, "Oh my Gods" and "you must be nuts," she offered Cory a complimentary session and wished her luck.

Cory drove to the office to collect the mail her office mate had stacked on the desk. There were tons of announcements for continuing education courses, bills, and letters from nosey insurance companies demanding additional information about patients. Such requests angered her because they were designed to avoid the insurance company's financial obligation. She tossed advertisements into the recycling trash, slipped the journals into her briefcase and paid all the bills.

The following day, she took care of banking, passport and patient follow-ups.

She spoke to Allison in the afternoon. The young mother had trouble concentrating, was unable to eat or sleep, but the bulimia had disappeared. She found that inexplicable, but Cory ruled it an empty stomach. There was no digested food to throw up.

"I'm a mess. I've bitten my nails and my cuticles are bleeding."

"That's not nutritious, Allison. Increase the supplement. You're going through a tough time and need strength."

"It's good you called. I'd completely forgotten to take it. Thanks for reminding me. I'm so frightened. It's awful. Every evening I pace the floor of the children's rooms thinking of what I need to do. I must liquidate my assets for the ransom, but we haven't heard from the kidnappers. Hamid's tied to the phone for fear he'll miss their call. What are they waiting for?"

"Maybe they're trying to find out how much you're worth, or they want information from Hamid, perhaps his trade secrets."

"Of course! That's it! They must know about his work. He'd give it up for the kids. That means we can get them back!" The conversation ended on a hopeful note.

Cory had dinner with her children. They detected something different about her, but she said it was a work project that had consumed her. They seemed satisfied with her explanation and they agreed it was exciting for her to be in London for a few weeks helping a patient. They seemed proud of her work. After dinner they went back to their university housing.

She spent the rest of the evening on the phone with Ben. For her, just the sound of his voice was like making love.

Cory mentioned the phone call Betty had taken. Both she and Ben were clueless as to who the warnings were coming from.

Ben had learned that the kidnapping had been reported by the nanny and a witness to the local police who referred it to Scotland Yard, but Hamid refused to cooperate, alleging fear for the kids' safety. He wanted to pay the ransom and be done with it.

As to the poisoning investigation, Ben reported that the young Hispanic man had been fired from the inn due to alcoholism, and was ruled out as a suspect. Cory was right about him being Puerto Rican.

Ben made the arrangements for Cory to collect her ticket at Lindbergh Field the next day and fly to L.A. They planned to travel together for London in time for a morning arrival. A compassionate person at the Regional Passport office of the State Department had taken one look at Allison and her documentation, heard her tearful story and issued the passport on the spot. Allison showed her gratitude with an offer for a free week-end at Mattingly Manor. Sans powdery cinnamon buns, Cory hoped.

Investigation of Allison's household staff revealed a startling discovery: Her chauffeur had disappeared.

⸗20⸗

The news of the missing chauffeur and the anticipation of a long journey leading down strange alleys to find kidnapped children kept Cory wide awake most of the night. Ben called early in the morning to wake her up, but she was already in the kitchen, sipping a second cup of strong coffee and gulping down the oat bran flaxseed combination that promised strength, fortitude, lower cholesterol, and the runs.

"Something's turned up. We found the chauffeur, "Ben said.

"Great!"

"No. He and the car went missing yesterday, but later the police found the wreck. From what I've heard, someone rigged the car with a bomb. His charred body was found inside the car at the Presidio."

"Oh my God! Poor guy. Poor Allison. She knew him for years. And she could have been in the car, too. How's she holding up?"

"Surprisingly well."

"The chauffeur could have poisoned me. He had the opportunity and probably overheard me tell Allison my plan to visit the bed and breakfast that day. She'd given him the package of baked goods with my name on it, but before he brought it to the inn, he could have sprinkled arsenic on the buns."

"This doesn't make sense. He worked for Allison's family since she was a child."

"If the bomb was meant for Allison, it's good she's leaving."

"I'm not sure she was the target. If you're right, then whoever is behind this was afraid the driver would lead us to the bad guys or to Hamid or would spill other important information. Its clear there's more to this than kidnapped kids. I don't want you in danger, Cory. Better not go."

"But I want to help Allison."

"Last chance to back out Cory. I'll understand. Allison has shown more spunk than you'd imagine."

"When children's lives are at stake, it's amazing what strength parents muster. I want to help her and I want to be with you."

"That's all this mission requires of you."

"Not my little gray cells?"

"You're not Hercule Poirot."

"I know. I feel more like his side-kick."

"You're much more than that, sweetheart."

Cory sighed. "I'll meet you at LA.X International as planned, Ben." She hung up, tidied the kitchen and called her home security system with instructions.

Cory couldn't get the chauffeur out of her mind. She knew nothing about him, and didn't want to know if anyone would mourn him. She didn't want to feel the pain and had other things to deal with. Anxiety about the trip. Would it lead to finding the children alive? She forced herself to dismiss any other possibility.

After she completed her chores, the cab she had ordered drove up and they hit the freeway for the airport. An odd feeling crept over her. She had no idea how long she'd be away.

꞊21꞊

Cory had left ample time to make the flight, but when they ran into snarled ground traffic at the airport, she grew nervous and fidgety and drummed her fingers on her lap. The cab driver, a true professional, snaked through and dropped her at United. She caught the shuttle for the short flight to L.A.X.

She arrived early enough for a stroll to the British Airway terminal where she would meet Ben and Allison outside the Executive Club lounge. Rolling her carry-on behind her, she thought she spotted Ingrid and hurried to catch up with her, but when the woman turned her head, she was someone else. Besides, Ingrid was supposed to have changed her appearance. Perhaps Cory would never recognize her. What had happened to her and why didn't she have the courtesy to make contact with someone who had tried to help her?

The hike to British Airways turned out to be longer than expected, but good exercise before a long flight. When Cory spied Ben her heart took a spin. She felt like a goofy teen in love, rushing toward him and throwing herself into his embrace. They clung to each other like long-lost lovers, but they were in a public place in L.A., not in Paris. For a moment she had forgotten about Allison, but noticing her absence, Cory became alarmed. "Where's Allison?"

"In the restroom. She's very nervous. Thought she'd faint on the flight here. Hope she does better on the way to London with her therapist on board."

"I'll sit beside her. Although..."

"Yeah. Me, too, sweetheart. Can't wait to have you all to myself."

"Mind reader," she said.

Ben had no news about the investigation. Hamid hadn't heard from the kidnappers. He promised to send a courier to meet them at Heathrow at the 9:40 Friday morning arrival.

They chatted for about ten minutes and still no Allison. Worried, Cory took off to search for her.

Locating the nearest restroom, she called her name, but Allison didn't answer. Cory scanned the crowd in adjacent areas, assorted shops and restaurants, but no Allison. Cory had that same feeling in the pit of her stomach as if her own child had gone missing.

Cory hurried to Ben. "Can't find her," she said, panting.

"Take it easy, Cory. Maybe she didn't fancy waiting on a long line to drop her drawers and tried to find another place. If she isn't back soon, we'll have her paged." He glanced at his wristwatch. "It's only been about twenty minutes and this is a big place."

"Maybe she's waiting for the crowd in the restroom to evaporate so she can vomit in private."

"She could have gone in the first class lounge, but wanted to wait for you here with me. She seemed to be holding up until we got to the airport. Maybe fear of flying got to her."

"I think she can put up a good front, Ben. I never expect a quick cure. I'm not a magician."

"Yes you are," he whispered in her ear. "You can make a part of me levitate."

But raw fear mingled with her passion for Ben.

Allison had been gone for over half an hour and Ben had her paged. They waited ten more minutes, but she didn't respond. Cory made another frantic search of the restrooms.

After combing the area to no avail, she started back to Ben.

Allison was sitting beside him, her head between her knees.

"You had us worried, Allison. What happened to you?" Cory asked.

Allison raised her head. "I'm so sorry. I truly couldn't help it. I felt wretched thinking about my children. I'm worried sick over them. I had to buy something nice for them, so I canvassed the arcade until I found the right things. Suddenly, I felt so faint, the clerk took me in the back... someone came from First Aid. I'm so embarrassed."

"How do you feel now?"

"A bit better. I've got to get on that plane. Hamid expects me. We can't go through this without each other."

"Of course. When did you last eat?"

"I... don't remember."

"Let's get you some nourishment now." Ben stood. "There's plenty of food in the lounge. I'll take her there while you check in, Cory." He handed Cory her ticket." We'll meet you inside." He helped Allison to her feet, holding her elbow to steady her as they entered the lounge.

After Cory checked in, she was admitted to the inner sanctum of the well-appointed exclusive room where Allison munched on finger sandwiches and fresh fruit. She gulped a large glass of milk. "I'm feeling better now," she announced.

Ben busied himself examining the well-equipped room with all the conveniences of a fine home. Cory figured this first class trip cost Allison a pretty penny. Her wealth bought physical luxury, but given her current situation, no poor person would change places with her if they could. Bereft of her children, fearing for them, she sobbed intermittently. She broke out in a cold sweat. Cory sat next to her and patted her damp brow with a Kleenex.

"You're too good to me, Doctor Cohen."

"Please call me Cory. I prefer it."

"Okay. After you were poisoned from my pastries, I thought you wouldn't work with me anymore."

"I never thought you were responsible, Allison. I want to help you."

"I hope you're earning enough to make this worthwhile for you. Please keep track of every single bill you have on my account, no matter how small. I want to be sure you're reimbursed completely." Allison's business-like stance probably helped her to cope and feel in control.

"Money isn't my prime concern, Allison, it is helping you get through this difficult time."

"I know you're sincere. Can you believe it? Here I am thirty-five years old and this is my first airplane trip."

They chatted about first class air travel. Cory told her about the royal treatment she'd had when upgraded on a flight from London to Dallas with champagne flowing like water in crystal goblets, and the incessant presentation of edible delights. Cory suddenly felt silly mentioning food to a woman with a serious eating disorder.

"This flight should be pleasant. Comfy seats, movies, the latest magazines, and you've got Ben and me, Allison."

"It's none of my business, but it's easy to see you're truly in love with each other."

Cory felt her face begin to redden.

"It's the same with Hamid and me."

"We're fortunate in that way," Cory said.

Allison's eyes moistened. She reached into her purse and pulled out a linen handkerchief with her initials embroidered on the edge.

Cory hadn't seen one like it since she was a young child. She figured Allison's was an heirloom.

"Oh, I want to show you what I picked up for the kids." She rooted through her purse and pulled out a small parcel. "Look," she said, whipping out two velvet hand puppets.

"They're adorable," Cory said, swallowing her tears."

Finally it was time to board. A young attractive flight attendant with an English accent directed them to large comfortable leather reclining seats and offered champagne, which they refused in favor of mineral water. Allison sat next to the window and Cory took the aisle seat beside her and adjacent to Ben.

Allison belted in and began to bite her nails, but stopped when Cory held her hand.

When the plane took off, Allison tightened her grip, surprising Cory with her strength. "I'm scared," she whispered.

"Flying will be a nice adventure."

"But I wouldn't be here if it weren't for my children," she sobbed.

"I know. This is your chance to get over your fear of flying. Concentrate on the comforts."

"I'll try," she said, squirming in her seat.

The trip was surprisingly pleasant, with slight turbulence. Allison remarked how much she enjoyed the flight attendant's solicitous attention. Ben donned headphones and dozed off until it was time to examine the menu. And what a menu it was, with abundant splendid choices and an extensive wine list.

Allison decided on grilled prawns and chicken with spicy Arabic sauce, saffron rice and French beans. Cory selected marinated salmon to start, followed by North Sea cod with yogurt dressing. Ben dug into a man-sized portion of thick moist steak. He sipped red wine.

For dessert, Allison spooned up the cappuccino mousse and asked for seconds. Grandma would have been proud of Cory's choice of fresh fruit.

Wisely, Allison refused the movie. The plot, concerning two children estranged from their father, would have ripped her apart. She dozed off clutching her children's velvet hand puppets to her bosom.

The commodious seats and accouterments allowed them to sleep well.

Awakened by early morning sunrise sending bright streaks through the edges of the cabin windows and the scent of rich coffee and croissants baking, Allison stirred. "First night with no nightmares and not only that, but I wasn't as frightened as expected." She excused herself to use the restroom.

Ben yawned. "Sleep well, sweetheart?"

"Uh-huh. And you?"

"Not bad. How'd she do?"

"Really well. I hope she won't get rattled during landing. It's scary for first time passengers."

Shortly after breakfast, the pilot announced their descent. A look of terror emerged on Allison's face. She gripped Cory's hand.

"This is normal. The pilot has done this many times. Breathe normally and concentrate on the rhythm and flow of your breath," Cory advised.

They landed at Heathrow, far busier than most international airports and replete with foreigners in native garb. Africans, Indians, Europeans—a babble of strange sounds, a cacophony of color.

They joined a long line at customs, presented their documents, answered a few questions and had their passports stamped. Off they went to look for the courier Hamid had promised to send. They stood near the crowded British Airways desk and read the signs carried by a huge parade of couriers. None of them bore Allison's name.

At ten thirty, Ben asked at the airline desk whether anyone had called for them, but no one had.

Allison called Hamid. There was no answer. "My God! He must have gone to meet the kidnapper," she said.

At Ben's insistence, she called Pru-petrol and asked to be connected to Hamid Mekenian. "Hello, Allison here, she said. Her knees buckled as she dropped the receiver. Ben steadied her.

"That man said he was Hamid Mekenian, but I know my husband's voice. That wasn't him!"

=22=

"Could it have been a bad connection? Or the noise here? "Ben asked as he prepared to make a call.

Allison shook her head and sobbed. "No. I heard the voice clearly."

Ben closed the door to the phone booth and punched in some numbers while Allison and Cory continued to scan the area for the courier.

In a few minutes, Ben stepped out of the booth. "I spoke with someone at Scotland Yard and left a message for the investigator assigned to the kidnapping. A couple of detectives will meet us at the house by the time we get there. Let's go." He pushed their luggage cart. "We'll take the tube into town. It's faster than a cab."

Cory put her arm around Allison and tried to reassure her. "We'll get to the bottom of this. With Ben and Scotland Yard, you've got the best."

They made their way to the underground station below the terminal, and boarded a waiting train. Within the hour they were standing on a bustling central London street corner. A red double-decker bus passed.

Late morning dark gray clouds threatened rain. Ben hailed a black cab and in they piled. He gave the driver Hamid's address in South Kensington. Large drops of rain began to pelt the car. A stream of pedestrians rushed by, sheltered by their umbrellas.

Jet lag and riding on the left side of the street disoriented Cory. Combined with anxiety over recent events, these elements warred inside her like bitter enemies. Everything took on a weird dreamlike cast, including this case.

Allison gasped. "If someone's changed places with Hamid, Hamid could be dead! And the kids? What's happened to them?"

"Let's not assume the worst. We're going to find out," Cory said.

The taxi driver pulled up to the curb in front of a row of attached stately narrow houses with black lacquered front doors and brass numerals. The buildings were set back a few feet. Ben paid the driver and they hopped out. Allison pressed the bell for the manager. An older woman with tightly curled gray hair and small blue eyes opened the door a crack. "May I help you?"

Allison explained who they were, dug through her purse and removed her wallet. She slid out her family photo and handed it to the woman. "I'm truly worried about my children and husband. He was supposed to have someone meet us at the airport, but no one showed up."

"Just a minute, please," the manager said. "I need my spectacles." She opened the door wider and slipped her hand in her pocket. Sliding her granny type glasses onto the bridge of her nose, she scrutinized the photo and returned it to Allison. Just then a gray car rolled up and out stepped two men wearing raincoats. "Mr. Fortuna?" the taller of the two asked.

"Yes." Ben extended his hand.

"Chief Inspector Wallace, here and Detective Sergeant Morton, Scotland Yard." The men shook hands and gave a cursory glance at each other's ID.

"Gentlemen, this is my associate, Cory Cohen. And this is Allison Mattingly, the children's mother."

The inspector flashed his badge at the manager. She turned and said, "Very well, then. Do come in."

They followed her upstairs.

"When did you last see Mister Mekenian?" Ben asked the manager.

"Just before I went on holiday, a fortnight ago. I came back last night," she replied.

"Who lived in this flat?" The inspector asked the woman as she unlocked the door to the flat.

"The gentleman and his children and Molly McBride, their nanny. They're a well-behaved lot for youngsters, not like some I could mention."

They entered the neatly furnished apartment.

"Thank you. That will be all, madam," the inspector said.

"HAMID," Allison shouted, running through the rooms. "Where are you?" There was no response.

Watching her, Cory felt dizzy. There was nothing to do while they inspected the premises. Cory plopped down on a chair and closed her eyes. She heard doors and drawers squeak open and slam shut.

"No clothes. No personal effects. Nothing. They've gone," Ben said.

"No! It can't be. Why? Where?" Allison sobbed.

"Madam, I'm sorry, but I think your husband is playing a hoax on you," the inspector said. "I understand that you are in the process of divorce and he could be subjected to prosecution in your country for removing the children from you. When he heard you were coming, he cleared out."

"Wait a minute, Inspector. This couple was planning to reconcile. Mister Mekenian promised to return to the states with the children, but they were kidnapped before he could do so. That's why we're here. I believe he's been abducted," Ben said.

"Makes no sense, Mr. Fortuna."

"Haven't you questioned the nanny about the kidnapping?" Ben asked.

"Yes. She confirmed it, but I think it was staged. The father refused to cooperate with us and evidently moved. This is a legal matter best pursued by California and no longer our concern." He started out the door, the sergeant following him.

"Please listen to me," Cory said. "Hamid Mekenian has an important position at Pru-petrol in London. When his wife called there for him a few hours ago, a man answered with his name, but he wasn't her husband. Doesn't that sound suspicious?"

"Indeed, but perhaps someone played a prank. Subsequent to your call to me, I phoned Pru-petrol and was told Mister Mekenian was sent to France on business yesterday."

"That's impossible," Allison said. "He'd have told me."

"Apparently there's much he has not told you, Madam."

"Inspector, will you provide us the nanny's address, please?" Ben asked.

The sergeant thumbed through a little notebook. "I have it, sir." He scribbled in his pad, ripped out the sheet of paper and started to hand it to Ben.

The inspector shot him a piercing glance. "All right, sergeant. Give it over. Sorry, but we cannot do more for you." He turned on his heel and the two men left the flat. Allison buried her face in her hands and sobbed.

"I think we should stay here. I'm going to see the manager," Ben said.

In a few minutes he returned. "The flat's ours indefinitely. Hamid's paid until the end of the month. Now, the two of you better get some shuteye. I'll be back later."

Cory nodded, shuffled into a bedroom, sank on the bed and crashed.

She awakened in darkness, for the moment unaware of the time or place. The glimmer of a distant street lamp illuminated Ben sleeping beside her. She heard muffled whimpers from the adjacent room. Allison.

To avoid disturbing Ben, who despite jet lag, had admirably gone right to work, Cory slowly slipped off the bed and closed the door behind her. She padded barefoot on the cold floor into Allison's room, lit by a bedside lamp. She was huddled at the far edge of the bed in a fetal position. Cory sat beside her and smoothed her hair. "I know this is difficult, Allison, and I don't mean to be a Pollyanna, but I believe we'll find Hamid and the kids, safe."

"I truly pray so, Cory. Look what I found here." In her palm lay a child's hair barrette shaped like a pink bow. "It's Shara's favorite." She wept.

Cory choked back tears and offered to see if there was any tea.

She found her way into the kitchen and flipped on the ceiling light. The sparsely stocked pantry contained a canister of Brooke Bond tea, sealed boxes of corn flakes and oatmeal and a new jar of marmalade. She heated a kettle of water and opened the refrigerator door. Ben must have been to the market. Fresh cartons of eggs, milk, and a sealed cheese bar, and wheat bread occupied a shelf. A net bag of oranges lay on the counter. Cory popped two slices of bread in the toaster and prepared English style tea. After setting the table, she tiptoed toward Allison's room. Allison had just come out of the bathroom and was dressing when Cory caught a glimpse of her nude skeleton-like body. Alarmed at the sight, Cory gasped, and then tip-toed away, hoping Allison hadn't heard her.

Soon, Allison shuffled into the kitchen. "Something smells good." She sat at the table, spread the ginger marmalade on the toast, filled a bowl with dry cereal and milk and much to their mutual delight, began to eat. Cory poured tea and joined her for breakfast—or was it dinner? Well, it was their first meal of the day.

"Ben must have come back while I slept. I didn't hear him. Did you?" Allison asked.

"No. I've no idea how long ago I crashed, but I feel refreshed. How about you, Allison?"

"I must have been emotionally and physically exhausted, because I drifted off right away too. I do feel better. I think we slept about ten hours, judging from the wall clock."

Cory left her in the kitchen drinking her second cup of tea while she attended to her morning rituals. Ben was still sleeping when someone knocked on the door.

"Don't open it, Allison," Cory whispered.

Cory looked through the peephole and saw a young woman carrying a bucket of cleaning supplies. "Who's there?"

"Peggy Ryan come to do your flat."

Cory hesitated, but figuring the maid might be able to provide information, she opened the door.

Peggy, a young woman with auburn hair and freckles, stared at Cory. "Who are you?" she asked.

"A friend of Mister Mekenian's wife."

Just then Allison presented herself and the woman said, "Oh, yes. I recognize you. Just like your pictures all over this place." She looked around. "But they're gone! Oh, dear me!"

"My husband took them with him. He had to travel for his work, but he'll be back." Allison was one heck of a liar.

"It's a shame you just coming from the states and all." She shook her head. "Where are the children?"

"They're with him," Cory said. "Would you like some tea?" Our friend is sleeping and I don't want the vacuum to wake him."

"Sure and that's nice of you. I could be doing with a cuppa before I start my cleaning. Leave the hoovering for next time."

Congenial as would-be roommates, they joined her at the table.

"It's lovely to work here. Molly and me, we're chums. During tea break we play games with the children. The mister is a fine one to be sure and loves you, me dear—talks about you all the time to the children—it's Mummy this and Mummy that. Proper little darlings they are."

Tears rolled down Allison's cheeks, but she was quiet.

"When did you last see Molly?" Cory asked.

She rubbed her chin. "Let me think, it must be two weeks gone. Me old mum's ailing and I didn't work last week. Me days for the mister are Tuesday and Saturday. Molly, she's off Thursday and

Sunday. Sometimes she and I spend Sundays together. Maybe she'll be at church tomorrow."

"Which church is that?" Cory asked.

"Saint Bridget's."

"If you see her, would you please ask where she's working now? I'd like to meet her and give her a present from the states for taking such good care of my children."

"Sure and I will, madam."

"What does Molly look like?" Cory asked.

Ben, clean shaven, hair damp strolled into the kitchen. "May I join you?" He poured himself a cup of tea. "Eggs anyone?"

The maid stood. "Good day to you, sir? I'll be starting on the bathrooms now and then give the fridge a do." She started to march off, stopped and turned around. "That Molly, she's about my height, got brown hair, green eyes. Come to think of it. She looks like me, but she's a mite slimmer." She patted her hips.

"Oh, Peggy," I called. "Is Molly McBride her full name?"

"As far as I know, it is."

Cory turned to Ben. "We've had breakfast, but I'll boil two eggs for you."

"Thanks. What have you learned?"

"That Hamid is in love with Allison, and Molly, the nanny may be at Saint Brigit's tomorrow, in case you haven't contacted her yet."

"Good lead. Molly's now living at her new employer, but I couldn't get the address."

"Let's go to the church service," Cory said. "If Peggy's there, she'll introduce us to Molly and you can take it from there."

"Good work, detectives." Ben said.

After breakfast, he took out three tiny phones and handed them out. "I picked this up for us yesterday. They're called mobile phones here. Take this with you so we can keep in touch. He handed them cards on which he'd printed the emergency phone number 999 and each of their mobile numbers.

≠23≠

Church services started at nine o'clock and they were ready. Cory wore the only dress she had packed, a simple gray affair. She pulled her hair back into a French knot and donned a pair of pearl earrings. Allison said she felt uncomfortable going into the church and preferred to wait with Ben on a bench outside.

Cory entered the stone-covered chapel fifteen minutes before the service. Sunlight filtered through the multi-colored stained glass windows. Worshippers were already seated. After vainly scanning the pews for Peggy, Cory parked herself on a rough-hewn seat at the end of the back row. Heads turned and people stared at her, a newcomer. There she was feeling out of place, an American Jew with an Asian face, in this quaint neighborhood church. If anyone were to ask her questions, she would say she heard this was a friendly place where she hoped to meet Molly McBride.

The service started, but Peggy failed to show. She may have been needed at home. She had said her mother was ill. Cory's eyes wandered from the hymn book to the congregation. Spying several possible women who could be Molly, she waited impatiently for the sermon to end. She tried to pay attention to the message, but the priest's Irish brogue enthralled her. Words rolled from his tongue like poetry.

Finally, the service finished and people, some laughing, others whispering, made their way out the open door. Cory pretended to look for something inside her purse in order to delay her departure and to observe the women she wanted to approach. One possible held hands with a man on one side and a child on the other. Wrong woman. Another appeared grim, not the sort she had imagined, but she went up to her. "Excuse me; I'm looking for Molly McBride."

"And what would you be wanting with her?"

"I have special regards from the States. Are you Molly?"

"No. Sorry madam."

"Thank you."

Two down, and one to go. Cory rushed toward the door in pursuit of the last possibility. "Molly," she called, but the woman didn't turn around.

Father O'Malley stood at the door. He took her hand in both of his and welcomed her warmly. She asked if he'd seen Molly McBride, but he shook his head.

Downcast, Cory walked slowly toward the bench.

"No luck, huh?" Ben said.

"That's right."

"Thanks for trying," Allison said.

"Let's go. There are other leads. Yesterday I found out Molly hangs out in a local pub," Ben said. "Today's her day off and maybe we'll get lucky. It's a nice walk from here."

Unlike Cory's mood, which mirrored Allison's, the weather was sunny and mild.

"If she wasn't in church this morning, maybe she won't be in the pub either," Allison said.

"Maybe she didn't feel religious this morning. Let's try the pub," Ben said. "It'll be an interesting experience."

O'Neill's was on the corner of a busy street. "Maybe they cater to a literary crowd," Cory said.

Ben laughed. "I don't think so. It could be the owner's name. Pubs differ in food and the type of people who frequent them. This one has a working class crowd and can get rowdy."

Surrounded by shrieks of laughter from several tables, Cory could hardly hear Ben. An attractive display of casseroles on a counter made her mouth water, but when the barkeep shouted the contents, she declined. No sausages or ground meat for Cory. Allison and Cory ordered the ploughman's lunch. Ben asked for bangers and mash. They waited on barstools around a small varnished wood table and watched the swift chef prepare their orders. Ben took a swig of draft bitter and Allison and Cory followed suit. The food arrived and Ben dug into his sausages and mashed potatoes. Allison stared at her plate and poked at the chutney.

"It's nice with cheese," Cory said, stabbing her fork into a pickled onion as if it might roll off the plate without warning.

"I had a big breakfast and am not very hungry. One meal a day is usually sufficient. Under other conditions, I'd enjoy this place, but... "

"Of course, Allison, I know it's hard, but distract yourself with the novelty here." An appropriate comment, but inane, Cory thought. It was hard to conceal her feelings of futility too. Ben kept busy scarfing his food and occasionally scanned the joint. When he finished lunch, he got off his stool and worked the room like a consummate politician. He appeared confident in his ability to make people trust him. What a splendid con man he could be. From out of nowhere, it made her question the depth of his feelings for her.

Grandma's voice cautioned her with one of her clichés:" Cory, shaina n'shuma, judge others by their deeds, not their words."

Ben returned to their table, a satisfied smile on his face. "A small success. Let's go and I'll tell you about it."

"Success means finding Hamid and the kids alive and well," Allison said.

"We're getting closer. I've confirmed what I suspected. Molly may be with your family."

"What? Please, Lord! Where are they?"

"I'm trying to find out. Yesterday I located the employment agency where Molly's registered. They'd set her up for an appointment with a family who asked for her specifically because of Hamid Mekenian's recommendation. The family was living at a hotel in the West End and the kids are the same ages as yours."

"What does this mean?" Allison asked.

"I went to the hotel, but they'd checked out. I showed a photo of your family to a chambermaid and she recognized them as the people who'd stayed in Room three-oh-three."|

Allison crossed her hands over her chest. "Oh my Lord!"

"I have a suspicion. Listen, Molly's a creature of habit. Every Sunday, she goes to church, and then joins her friends at the pub that we just left, but not today. Her friends said she's very consistent and they're worried. I think she may be held captive with Hamid and the kids."

"Why?"

"Whoever abducted them may want to keep them comfortable. A good sign. They may not be in real danger and will be released when their mission is accomplished."

"What mission?" Cory asked.

"You can't be sure of any of this. You must find them! Now!" Allison sobbed.

"The trail is still warm and I'm on it. I'll catch up with you later at the flat. Listen to Cory and try to distract yourself, Allison. Go sightseeing together."

"Sightseeing? That's not why I'm here!"

"Ben's right, Allison, you need a distraction." *I do, too*, Cory thought, selfishly. "Will you call us on the mobile and let us know what you're up to?" she asked.

"Yes. You'll probably get a cockamamie message from me." He hailed one of those black square-shaped London cabs and off he went.

"What does that mean?" Allison asked.

"Ben's shorthand for mixed-up. He's working hard for you. "Let's go to a quiet, calm place."

She stared at the sidewalk. "I don't feel like doing anything, Cory. I'm too worried."

"That's the point. Worrying won't change things. It's counterproductive, makes you feel worse. We may as well take in the sights." Cory handed her a tourist guide she had picked up at the airport.

They leaned against the wall and Allison stared at the book cover. Finally, she thumbed through it. "I guess we can take the tube to Russell Square and see the British Museum."

Cory nodded as they strolled toward the underground station. They boarded the tube and sat in silence. Allison's furrowed brow and blood-shot eyes signaled worry and fear. Cory figured Allison had chosen the museum as a favor to her. If Allison were alone, she'd probably curl up in bed and weep.

Cory glanced at the enigmatic faces of passengers who seemed lost in thought. She passed the time wondering what each could be thinking and the stories that made up their lives. Their lovers or desire for one, their parents, children, bosses, what to prepare for dinner or how to get even with a rival.

At Russell Square, they trotted off the train. Allison linked Cory's arm as they ambled towards the wide, gray stone building with a vast verdant green lawn.

Near the entrance to the Egyptian Sculpture Gallery, Cory examined the famed Rosetta Stone. She was transfixed until she became aware of Allison who seemed totally detached from the surroundings.

"Perhaps you'll find the sculptures of the Parthenon and the Greek antiquities interesting, Allison." Cory hoped to distract her from her present worries, but she accepted it as a futile gesture.

"I see why this is one of the most famous museums in the world," Allison said. She began to express an interest and knowledge of ancient cultures which surprised Cory. There was more to Allison Mattingly than she had imagined.

They strolled through the museum, but the initial spark of interest did not last and her blank facial expression returned. It was apparent she'd gone along with the program to please her therapist, but it failed to shake her loose from her worries. Ben meant well, but anyone in Allison's circumstances would have a hard time.

"I'm truly sorry, Cory, but I'm tired. I'd like to leave now."

Cory suggested afternoon tea, but Allison said she was in no mood for cucumber sandwiches and sweets and was now ready for a decent meal. Cory was surprised at the anorexic woman's sudden interest in eating something substantial.

"I'd like to go here," she said, pointing to a page in the guide book. "Do you think your stomach can handle it?"

"I'm sure they'll serve rice and veggies."

Back on the tube they went to the middle of Soho in search for what was touted as "one of London's best Southeast Asian restaurants." Allison peered at shop windows and old buildings and seemed to enjoy being part of the crowd and excitement of London. Cory was surprised and pleased to see her lively for a change, even if only momentarily.

They dined at a long wooden table in a two-story noisy, crowded restaurant decorated with paper lanterns. As Allison dug into her dish with gusto, Cory watched with delight. The rice and vegetables with bits of spicy shrimp made her thirsty. She topped off the meal with a large dose of mineral water.

They hailed a taxi back to the flat. Allison unlocked the door just as the phone started to ring. "Please get it, Cory."

Cory raced to pick up the receiver.

"Is it on?" Ben asked.

"Light's off."

"Okay, I've got a lead. Don't tell Allison, but there's a woman involved."

Cory tried to hide her surprise. "We just got in. Everything's fine. We went to the British Museum and had dinner in Soho."

"She ate?"

"And how!"

"She had an appetite? Well... I have one, too. For you, sweetheart."

Every time Ben did his Bogart shtick, his words massaged her pleasure zones. She paused to separate her physical feelings from her intellect.

"What are you thinking about?" Ben asked.

Momentarily, she had forgotten about Allison and her problems and Ben's news of a woman involved with Hamid. "It can wait. Anything else, Ben."

"Yeah. You seem to have cooled off. What's wrong?"

Cory whispered, "Not a good time to discuss it. She's here."

"You had me worried for a minute. I'll catch you, later. Ciao."

Cory was weary, but had a hard time falling asleep. Not only was she worried about the outcome of this case, but she had professional concerns. Respected for her ethical behavior, she had to deal with a breach that began with sharing the flat with Allison. A psychologist must establish boundaries, but Cory's had eroded. Circumstances had changed her role to that of supportive friend, but she was a *paid* friend and that didn't set well with her. She realized she was hard on herself and was doing what had to be done. Unusual circumstances require unusual responses. Ethics, shmethics! As long as she was a benefit to the patient.

When Ben had asked for help with this case, she flew to him without hesitation. Had she responded too quickly because of her own personal needs rather than considering what would be best for the patient?

She wrestled with the possibility that she had fallen for a charming con artist, but then regarded it as a bizarre thought borne of guilt for being happy with Ben when poor Allison was miserable. It was unfair to construct such an equation.

She heard Allison wretch in the bathroom. She wanted to stop her and to offer comfort, but, she was too tired to leave the bed and rationalized that Allison couldn't be comforted. The eating disordered patient had moved a couple of steps forward, only to regress. Typical, from what she knew about the disorder.

Before falling asleep, she reassured herself that she was doing her best with Allison and that should count for something.

Sometime later, the sound of running water awakened her. Ben was back and she longed for him. He slipped into bed. She rolled over and wrapped herself around him. "I want you," she whispered.

It was obvious he wanted her, too. They clung to each other like peanut butter and jelly and it was just as sweet.

Later, he whispered, "There was a woman with Hamid and the kids at the hotel. They'd registered under false identities with a phony New York address. They had U.S. passports and paid in cash. At least we know the kids are safe."

"I don't get it," she said softly. If Hamid's involved with another woman, why would he pretend to the maid that he was in love with his wife and why tell Allison he wanted reconciliation?"

"Perhaps that's true, but this woman has some sort of hold on him."

"Will you tell Allison about the woman?"

"For the moment, I'll tell her everything, but that."What about Pru-petrol and this lie about sending Hamid to France?"

"Maybe it's not a lie."

Leaning on her elbow, she gazed at a streak of moonlight on Ben's face. "So why would someone who wasn't Hamid, say he was?"

"Tomorrow is Monday and I can scope out Pru-petrol. I've rented a car. Don't worry; I've driven on the wrong side of the road before."

"Yeah, when you've had one too many."

"You know me better than that."

"And I want to know you even better." She went back to sleep in Ben's arms.

≈24≈

Lost in thought on her way to the park for an early morning run, she had failed to look to the right before stepping off the curb. The blast of a car horn, the screech of brakes and an irate driver—his fist out the window, yelling at her, "Damn colonial!"

How did he know? Her sweatshirt blazoned with MADE IN AMERICA across her chest had provided the clue.

When she reached Kensington Gardens, where the nanny had been knocked down by the cyclist and the children kidnapped, she was glad that Allison wasn't with her. Cory needed a break from her and the grim situation. Allison seemed eager to be alone. Perhaps she wanted freedom to put her finger down her throat as she did last evening.

Ben had driven off early in the morning, to get the skinny on Pru-petrol.

Cory slowed her pace and began to power-walk when her mobile phone rang.

"It's Allison. I'm sorry to interrupt your run, but I don't feel well and I'm scared to be alone."

"Okay. I'm ten minutes away, Allison. Should you call nine-nine-nine?"

"No, I recognize it as my own anxiety."

Cory ran back, took the stairs two at a time and breathlessly hurled herself into the flat. Allison lay sprawled on the bed, panting, clutching her throat.

Cory tilted Allison's head back to open her airway. "Is that better?"

"Uh-uh," she said hoarsely.

"Did you vomit, Allison?"

Allison covered her face with her hands. "I tried. Nothing came out," she said, a tremor in her voice. "My throat feels like sandpaper."

Cory dashed into the kitchen and filled a large goblet with bottled water.

Allison raised herself on her elbows as Cory held the glass to her lips.

"I can't help it. I hurt so much inside over my children that when I throw up it makes me forget."

"Vomiting is not a solution. It's a problem."

"You're right. If I wasn't bulimic Hamid wouldn't have taken the children here. It's all my fault." She sobbed.

"That's not true. Your children could have been kidnapped in the states."

"What do you mean?"

"If the kidnappers want information from Hamid, the eating disorder is irrelevant."

She trembled. "I truly thought I was better, but it seems whenever I have a big meal, I feel I should throw up. Maybe it's a habit, or maybe it's my guilt and worry."

"Yes. It is a habit based on telling lies to yourself—that eating is bad and the antidote is to purge." You must counter those lies with truths. Eating is healthy. Purging is unhealthy. Make those words your mantra. Say them over and over again until they are no longer needed. It helps to remember that your kids need a healthy mother."

"I know. I truly do know." She turned on to her stomach and cried into her pillow.

Cory lightly massaged the woman's bony shoulders.

She missed her friend Betty and was tempted to call her for support, but a glance at her Timex showed it was the middle of the night in San Diego.

"I've disappointed you, Cory," Allison said.

"No, you've disappointed yourself and I'm frustrated with my inability to help you."

"But you have. Ben sent you to me for emotional support, and you do your job well. It would be much worse for me without you."

"It's not enough, Allison. I want to help you rid yourself of this foul disease that rots your teeth, screws up your electrolytes and hurts you in so many ways."

"I'll try to stop it for you," she said softly.

"If you won't do it for your kids and your husband, why would you do it for me? Is it because your mother was impossible to please? Perhaps you view me as your surrogate mother—one who wants to comfort you and is concerned with your welfare."

"Yes. That may be it. You're like the mother I wish I had. Is that strange?

"Often a therapist is viewed as a parent—with all the real and imagined flaws of the patient's parent. The psychological term for the experience is "transference.""

"Is that normal?"

"Those feelings and thoughts are common. Often, patients attribute to a therapist the qualities they wish they had in their own parent. They feel that in order to receive those qualities from the therapist, they must figure out what the parent-slash-therapist wants from them."

"That makes sense. What do you want from me?"

"Tell me when you're hungry and are trying to resist food."

"Okay. I'll truly try. What else?"

"Tell me when you want to throw up, and let me talk you out of it."

"I'll try that too." She sipped the water.

"Sorry. Try isn't good enough. I need a commitment from you."

"What if I get the urge when you're sleeping?"

"Wake me up."

"Or when you're on a run?"

"Call my mobile."

Allison smiled. "I guess you've got all the answers. You know, Cory, the problem may be my big appetite. When I eat too much I have to throw up. It isn't a physical thing, like I'm too full, but I feel it's wrong and bad to eat large quantities. To avoid it, sometimes I won't eat at all."

"Analyzing it, trying to understand yourself, is a very good start. I salute you, Allison."

Allison rose from the bed, smoothed the creases of her long wool dress and sauntered into the parlor, followed by her therapist.

They sat on opposite ends of the couch and discussed what was considered her misperception of quantity. Allison said she mentally calculated the fat and calorie content of everything she consumed. If she went above her limit, she'd vomit and fast for several days.

"Who sets these limits, Allison?"

"I do."

Cory shook her head. "Restaurants prepare an amount for the average palate—although some are more generous and others stingy, but let's look at what you see as average. You don't have double portions, do you?"

"No."

"You may think you're overindulging when you aren't. Food is necessary for survival. It isn't an all or nothing deal."

"Thank you. I'll remember that. Did Ben tell you his plan for today?"

"He drove off early this morning to check out Pru-petrol."

A terrified look spilled across her face. "No! He mustn't do that!"

"But why not?"

"I... I'm afraid."

"Of what?"

She hesitated. "I don't know."

Cory didn't believe her. Perhaps Allison's naiveté was one big act.

≈25≈

Cory came to a stalemate with Allison. She was tired of playing her nursemaid. Except for a brief run in the park, they hadn't been apart. The dark cloud of despair shrouding her had begun to attack Cory. She felt suffocated.

Weary too, of playing Doctor Watson to Ben's Sherlock Holmes, Cory longed to go off on her own and do a bit of snooping.

"Allison, I need to be alone for awhile. I'm taking a few hours off today. If you need to contact Ben or me, you have our mobile phone numbers."

"That's fine. I truly understand. I know I'm not the best company."

"I'm not accustomed to constant togetherness, Allison. Sometimes I crave solitude."

"Thanks for telling me. On your way back, would you please bring a newspaper?"

Well, at least she was interested in the news. Cory nodded and peered out the window. Although the sun made a valiant effort to push through a gray sky, she figured in case of a downpour, she'd better wear her Burberry raincoat. Besides, the garment made her feel she belonged in London and reminded her of an earlier visit.

"There's fruit and cheese for lunch, but maybe you'd like to take yourself to a cafe. Promise you'll eat and keep it down, Allison."

"I don't feel like going out. I'll try to eat here."

"Trying isn't good enough. You must commit."

"Yes, Doctor Cohen."

"So now you're getting formal with me, Allison?" Cory snickered, grabbing her purse.

"Oh! Sorry Cory." She smiled.

Exiting the building Cory felt like a recent prison parolee. Ah. sweet freedom.

She found her way to Trafalgar Square, a bustling area with traffic noise and a parade of pedestrians hastening about. Cory felt she had come alive. Tourists, cameras strapped to their shoulders, stopped to snap photos of the nearly two hundred foot column honoring Lord Nelson. Statues of lions guard the base. A swarm of pigeons pecked around the four bronze panels that depict naval battles against the French. The French and the Brits seem to continue their animosity to each other to this day.

Cory ambled to Liberty to check out their popular colorful silk scarves. They made fine gifts and were easy to transport. One scarf caught her eye. The design was exquisite. As she spread it out, the clerk said," You have excellent taste. This is one of *Ingrid's Images*. It is magnificent."

She wondered what had become of Ingrid. The woman had not made any contact with her. Cory was tempted to buy the scarf, but the price was out of her range. She decided to purchase five other scarves instead; the price of one of Ingrid's.

At a glance at her Timex, she realized she had taken more time than intended.

She rushed to the financial district where the offices of Rock Securities were located. An attractive blonde young woman clad in a red wool dress sat behind a granite counter sorting a stack of mail. She looked up and smiled. "May I help you?"

"Yes. I'm Doctor Cohen. I have an account with your firm in the States. Unfortunately, I haven't been able to reach Charles Anderson, my broker in your San Diego branch for a consultation. I'm considering an investment in a multinational company with offices here, but need more information. Would you kindly direct me to a broker?" She scribbled her account number on back of her card and handed it to the blonde woman.

"I'll fetch someone." The woman turned around the corner, leaving her station unattended.

The reception room was furnished in contemporary fashion with crimson tweed upholstered seating and sculptured halogen lighting. Cory sat next to a table and picked up a recent edition of *The Economist*.

Before she had time to read it, a short, squat man with a waxed mustache came her way. "Good morning. My name is Rodney Blair. Perhaps I can be of assistance. Please step into my office, Doctor Cohen."

She followed him into a cubicle the size of a broom closet, but it had a wide expanse of glass overlooking the street. Perhaps the window was a concession to claustrophobic clients. Blair seated himself behind a desk which dwarfed him. The ceiling light reflected off his bald pate.

She took the only available chair in the small room. "I'm considering an investment in Pru-petrol, but I want to research this company before making a decision, Mister Blair."

"Yes. Well, we can provide some information about the company immediately, but it would take some time to secure the last annual and most recent quarterly reports."

"How long?"

"Perhaps a week, or so." He straightened a stack of papers near the computer on his desk.

"That's unfortunate. You see, I'm prepared to make an investment here in a few days and hoped you could obtain such reports in haste for your preferred customers. Doesn't Pru-petrol have a London office?"

From a bookcase lining the wall, the broker thumbed through several shelves of volumes that resembled catalogues. "Ah, here we are," he said, opening one. He ran his finger down the page. "Yes. Pru-petrol is headquartered in France, but they do have a branch here. I will call both places and see if they can send one directly to you. May I have your address, madam?"

"I'm rarely there and would prefer it sent to you. I can wait in the reception room while you make the calls."

"Very well. I'll do it now."

Cory returned to the chair she had earlier vacated in the reception room. She tried to generate interest in the financial literature—an excellent antidote for insomnia, and started to nod off when Rodney Blair came into view.

"I'm dreadfully sorry, Doctor Cohen, but the reports you request are at Pru-petrol's headquarters in France and there was no one there to help me. I will have to phone later. Is there anything else I may do for you?"

"No. Thank you. How disappointing! I'll contact you in a day or so. Should you receive the information sooner, please call my mobile phone." She scribbled the number on back of her card and handed it to him.

"Very well, madam." The broker escorted her to the door.

She glanced at a wall clock and figured it was time to check on Allison. She punched in her number, but there was no answer. Maybe she was busy barfing in the bathroom.

Cory joined a pack of pedestrians rushing for lunch. Wondering what Allison was doing, she phoned again. Still no answer. Was she worrying needlessly? She's a grown-up. Yes, but a deeply troubled one. She was about to return to the flat when her mobile rang.

"Doctor Cohen, Rodney Blair here. I have Pru-petrol in France on the other line. They are ready to fax me the information you request if you will be specific."

"That's fine. I'd like their last quarterly report, the location of the wells and information about the backgrounds of the officers."

"That usually appears in the annual report."

"If they want my investment, they should include the information."

"Forgive my curiosity, but why is that relevant?"

"In addition to financial considerations, I frequently make investments by my feelings generated from an examination of the background and the photos of people in power in a company. This has worked well for me, so far."

"Yes. I see. They'll probably only send information on the wells currently in production. The material will be waiting for you to collect in the reception room."

"Thank you. That will be fine." She was tempted to say, Ta-ta, or Cheerio, but changed her mind.

Threading her way back through the crowded streets to Rock Securities took fifteen minutes.

An older man had replaced the attractive blonde receptionist at the counter. "May I help you?" he asked, peering over eye glasses perched at the tip of his nose.

She explained her mission and he handed her a large manila envelope which she tucked into her purse.

"Thank you. Please send my appreciation to Mister Blair for his expeditious service"

"Certainly, madam."

Cory wandered the sidewalk in search of a quiet pub where she could grab a bite, but "quiet pub" especially during lunch time, was an oxymoron. Eager to go through the contents of the envelope before she rushed back to the flat, she headed north to the National Gallery to treat herself to one of the greatest European art collections.

When she arrived, she was delighted to see that admission was free. That's Europe. One shouldn't have to pay a sum for culture, or health care for that matter, as we do in the States, she thought.

She had a good look around before wandering over to the museum's restaurant for lunch. There she opened the envelope and sorted through the contents. She pulled out a description of the oil-producing wells. Most, as she had expected, were located in Middle Eastern countries. Pru-petrol listed offices all over the world. This was a major, major company making tons and tons of money.

She was almost tempted to buy their stock, but she didn't like with whom they did business—countries that featured terrorism. She thumbed through papers until she found what she wanted: the photos and backgrounds of these zillionaires. She covered her mouth to stop from laughing. Half of those men resembled Mohammed, who come to think of it also resembled Saddam Hussein, the devil, once thought to have secret weapons of mass destruction.

The other half, apparently were European business men whose pin-striped suits fit them as well as did their names. There were several Dutch *Van this* and *Van that*, a couple of French, Pierre and Jacques, one Spanish, probably Catalan, Carles, and an Iranian, Kami. Some were geologists and petroleum engineers with advanced degrees. They certainly knew how to make money. Cory continued to peruse the papers hunting for possible useful information such as the folks who ran the show in London, but her search was futile.

She phoned Allison again. Still no answer. She began to worry and decided it was time to head back to the flat, but first, she'd call Ben.

"Where are you, Cory?"

"Why? Is something wrong?"

"Our gal called me earlier. She said you went out because you needed to be alone."

"I've called her a few times, but she doesn't pick up. I'm going to head back."

"It's probably a good idea—we know she's unstable."

"I had to get away from her for a few hours. I went to a brokerage house and got some info on the company. You know the one I want to invest in."

He understood that she didn't want to reveal too much on a mobile phone. "Oh that one. Is it worthwhile?"

"I hope you'll help decipher the financial stuff. It bores me. The company is multinational—huge holdings. On the annual report there are pin-up photos of the handsome guys in charge. By the way, why did she call?"

"She ordered me to stay away from you-know-where. I don't like this, Cory."

"Something's wrong there, Ben. Very wrong. She knows more than she's told us."

=26=

While traveling on the tube back to the Kensington flat, Cory listened to Ben on the mobile phone.

"I'm in the car with a pair of binoculars outside the parking lot of the company in question to see if I recognize anyone when the staff leaves."

"And if you do?"

"I'll follow."

Cory had visions of Ben dressed as Superman trailing Hamid's look-alike to a distant farmhouse where he would rescue the children. "How will we know when to expect you?"

"I'll call. Tell you what I'm up too. Listen, Cory. When you see our gal, you've got to convince her to cooperate."

The prospect gave Cory a queasy feeling. "Good luck. Ciao, Ben."

She watched several fellow passengers whispering into their mobile phones.

When cellphones first came out, Cory used to think people who spoke on them in public were showing off their importance, but now the device had gained usefulness for her. Mobile phones were more affordable and thus more ubiquitous abroad than in the States in their developmental years. Sensitive to privacy, she worried about the penetrability in the new technology, especially something personal such as mobile phone usage. She found herself dwelling on such mundane things to avoid confronting a painful suspicion about Allison.

Conflicted because she cared for her, Cory didn't want to accept the possibility that Allison might be untruthful, but it seemed she knew more about her husband's business than she'd let on. Why else would she try to thwart Ben's investigation? Did she know it wouldn't help him find the children? What was it she was afraid he'd find out?

And where was she this afternoon? Cory hoped to find out when she got to the flat.

She stepped out of the station into pouring rain, thankful for her raincoat and her umbrella stashed in her shoulder-strap purse. She tugged it open as a gust of wind blew the rain, soaking the top of the newspaper and the manila envelope that poked out of her purse. She jumped over a puddle, landing in another, and struggled to keep the umbrella erect. Her shoes sopped, squishing with each step.

Finally, she reached the apartment. She kicked off her shoes, unlocked the door and called out for Allison. No response. Her heart pound in panic as she knocked on Allison's door.

A feeble voice answered, "Is that you, Cory?"

"Phew," Cory sighed, slipping off her soaked coat. "Glad you're home. I was worried when you didn't answer the phone. Where were you?"

"Please come in," she said in a girlish voice.

Cory opened the door and found her stretched out on the bed covered with a blanket. Her hair looked damp.

"Did you get caught in the rain, too, Allison?"

She raised herself up on her elbows. "I don't want to be mean; Cory, but you left me alone. You didn't tell me where you were going, so I think I have the same right." She pouted.

Allison's juvenile response surprised Cory. Apparently she had grown dependent upon Cory and related to her as the good mother she wished she'd had. Allison construed Cory's time off as rejection and abandonment. Much as she most likely felt when her mother had left her for the country club. Given her present circumstances, she needed more from Cory than a therapist was ready to supply. Cory acknowledged that she had taken on this assignment without much thought of the demands. Now, she had to deal with picking up the pieces and putting them together.

"Well, Cory, you're just standing there. Say something, please."

"If you didn't want me to leave, I wish you'd have said so."

"You didn't give me a choice. It was so sudden; I didn't have time to think about it. My mother never prepared me when she was going out. She'd just leave. No notice. Poof and she was gone."

"I'm sorry, Allison. I should have been more sensitive to your feelings. Do you think telling you I needed a few hours by myself was unreasonable?

"No, I guess not." Playing the role of dutiful daughter, she said what she thought her parent slash therapist wanted to hear. Cory understood why Allison kept her feelings buried and the possible connection to her vomiting.

Or was her present behavior a diversion from offering an explanation for preventing Ben's investigation of Pru-petrol? Allison would have to say something about it when pressed.

"Okay. It's time we clear things up, Allison."

"What do you mean?"

"Now that I know you don't want to be left alone. If I need a few hours off Ben can stay with you while I take off. Is that acceptable?" Cory thought perhaps Allison would consider Ben a strong, protective, intelligent man—as her good father.

"Yes. That would be fine. Truly it would." Was she trying to convince herself?

"Where is he now?" she asked.

"Last I heard, he was trying to chase a lead to your children."

"Not at Pru-petrol, I hope."

"Why, not?"

"Uh--I can't say."

"You can't or you won't?"

She bit her lower lip. "I've been sworn to secrecy."

"Don't you want to find Hamid and the children?"

"Of course."

Cory held her hands. "Look, Allison, we can't help you without your cooperation."

Allison pulled her hands away and buried her face in them. "I don't know what to do. I'm so confused."

"I hope you realize you can trust us. Why would we come all this way to help you?"

"That's why this is so hard for me. I truly do trust you, but if I tell you, it could make it worse. I'm afraid my family will be killed."

"Killed? By whom?" Cory whispered. "Someone at Pru-petrol?"

Allison shrugged and scanned the room. "Ben checked for bugs here, didn't he?"

"Yes. It's clear. He checked, but it was before you went out today."

"Just to rent a television," she responded as though to an accusation.

Cory noticed a portable TV perched on the end table.

"Please Allison, for heaven's sake, tell me."

"I want to, but I swore my loyalty. To Hamid. To our government."

"Does that mean Hamid's an agent?" Cory whispered.

Allison shook her head.

Cory's feet were cold and wet and she wanted to take care of herself, but it wasn't a priority. She hugged herself for warmth.

"Are you okay, Cory? You're shivering. And wet. I'll make tea while you tend to yourself, and then we'll talk. I promise. She slid off the bed and gently pushed Cory out of her room.

≈27≈

Cory marveled, noticing how quickly they had changed places—the patient becoming the caring parent of her therapist.

Hoping fervently that Allison would reveal more and wouldn't have time to change her mind, Cory dashed into the bathroom and took the quickest shower of her life.

Wearing sweats and a towel wrapped turban style around her head, Cory settled in a kitchen chair with a cup of Earl Grey tea cradled in her hands. Allison sat across the table sipping the brew.

"Well, Cory, here goes. Last year, Hamid worked for Pru-petrol on a special project in the Middle East. Although he had to leave us for a few months, he was thrilled for the chance to test a system he'd worked on for years."

"What kind of system?"

"An advanced method for reinvigorating old oil wells. It's superior to anything used before and it's environmentally safe."

"That's quite an achievement."

"It truly is. Well, anyway, while he was on the site checking out some wells, he overhead two Pru-petrol officials discussing a plot to attack a nation, an ally of the United States that made him reconsider announcing his process to Pru-petrol.

"What did he do?"

"Well, he told someone he knows well, an important person in our government. The man advised him to continue his work and not breathe a word about his find to anyone.

"So this means he's an informant for the CIA?"

"Please, Cory, this must be kept highly confidential"

"Keeping secrets is what I do for a living, Allison.

Don't worry; Ben isn't interviewing anyone at Pru-petrol. He's a professional. You know his background."

"Yes. That's why I hired him. "That's somewhat of a comfort."

"Most likely someone is after Hamid's process. That's why the children were kidnapped. The ransom is a trade: Kids for secrets."

Fear and fatigue spilled across Allison's drawn face.

"My guess is that unless Ben rescues them first, Hamid and the children will remain captives until he reveals his technique. I bet his captors are waiting for another petroleum engineer to arrive so Hamid can explain his method to him. He's a smart man and he'd make a deal to assure the children's safety before giving anything away."

"I pray for my family's safety."

"This situation is hard on you, Allison, but I feel certain it'll be resolved soon. Do you have a contact person to call in case of trouble?"

"I have a number in San Francisco, but was told to use it only if I haven't heard from Hamid after seventy-two hours." She checked her watch. "That's just about now."

Reaching into the pocket of her brown corduroy jumper, she whipped out a card and limped toward the table where the mobile was perched. She picked it up and punched in a long string of numbers. She read some identification off the card and then proceeded to give the phone numbers for the flat and mobile before she hung up.

"Have you done this before?" Cory asked.

"No, but Hamid told me to follow the instructions on this card and to leave the information on the voice mail. Now, tell me exactly what is Ben doing at Pru-petrol?"

"He's staking out your husband's look-alike."

"What? I don't understand."

"Back in San Francisco, we saw a man who bore a striking resemblance to your husband. Remember we asked you if he had any local relatives?"

She stared at Cory. "Oh, yes."

"Well, we noticed this man on several occasions. In fact, your neighbors spotted him lurking outside your house peering through the windows. At first glance, they thought he was Hamid, but you'd told them he was abroad. They described him as a bit shorter than your husband and reported him to the police as a prowler."

"Why didn't they tell me?"

"I don't know, Allison, but Ben got this information directly from the people next door to you. Perhaps they didn't want to scare you," Cory said, pouring more tea. "It turns out that someone we knew also recognized this man as a friend of her husband, a Jordanian diplomat in New York. She said the man called himself Mohammed Daqamseh. Does that mean anything to you?"

Allison paled and began to tremble, but said nothing.

"Please answer me. Do you know this man?"

She shook her head. Apart from the steady rhythm of raindrops striking the window, all was quiet.

Finally, she spoke. "His name doesn't ring a bell, but to think someone has spied on us—someone who resembles Hamid, well, that's truly frightening. She rested her chin in her hand. "Wait a minute! Come to think of it, there is someone who may be a dead ringer for Hamid—his cousin, Mosen Mekenian."

"Have you ever met him or seen his photo?"

"No, but I imagine they'd look alike since their fathers are brothers and their mothers are sisters—actually two identical twins married two identical twins. But we understood that Mosen has never left Jordan."

"You can't be sure. What can you tell me about him?"

"Let's see," she said, tapping her thin fingers on the table. "The family is Armenian, but lived in Iran for a long time until they relocated to Jordan. I think Mosen grew up there. They had a lot of oil money. Hamid and Mosen's fathers were petroleum engineers and I think Mosen is a geologist."

"They have a lot in common."

"True. They're close in age, too. Hamid always felt Mosen was jealous of him. He blamed his mother for praising him too highly to Mosen's mother."

"Hamid is insightful."

She nodded. "The family had a falling out over some political differences. When we married, Hamid tried to patch things up by inviting them to our wedding. They wrote an apology for not attending, and sent us a very expensive gift. Hamid accepted it as an attempt to bury the hatchet."

"Do you know if Mosen ever traveled to the States?"

"No, but I'd imagine if he did, he would've contacted Hamid. Despite their rivalry, they have a strong sense of family."

She sipped her tea. "If you think this Mohammed is really Mosen, then that's truly scary!" She began to pace the room, crossing her thin arms over her sunken chest.

Allison mobile rang and she made a dash for it. Her back was toward Cory, she spoke softly and Cory couldn't hear. In a few moments, she slammed the receiver down.

"What happened, Allison?"

"They're so matter-of-fact—not an ounce of compassion. They'll check into it and call when they have information. They asked me to call again if something turns up. They don't care. Truly they don't." She burst into tears.

Cory grabbed a tissue from the box on the kitchen counter and handed it to her. Allison mopped her eyes and rested her head in her hand.

"You probably spoke to a clerk who thinks it's best to maintain emotional distance. I know. That's a poor excuse, but at least now the agency can get on it."

She nodded, brushing back wisps of hair that had fallen over her drawn face.

"Hamid always made me feel safe." Allison closed her eyes, perhaps remembering better times. "If only he'd phone. When we lived together he called daily and sometimes several times a day. And when we separated he continued the pattern. It wasn't just so the kids could speak to me, but he wanted to, also." She sniffled. "I told you, we're very close."

Cory believed her, but wondered about the woman with Hamid and the kids. Was it really Hamid? She worried about Ben, an experienced agent in the thick of his trade, but with no back up.

≠28≠

They hadn't moved from the kitchen table where they sat staring at each other.

Cory had questions and she wanted answers. She continued to grill Allison.

"Do you know if Hamid works closely with his colleagues?"

"Do you mean physical proximity?"

"Yes, face-to-face contact with co-workers?"

"Let me think a moment." She tapped her fingers on the table. "He told me most of his collaboration is on the computer. You see, Pru-petrol contracts with people for short term projects. I don't think there'd be much of a problem if someone took his place. But that person would have to be familiar with Hamid's work and be totally proficient in six languages."

"Six?"

"Uh-huh. Then again, I suppose Mosen's multi-lingual as well. I just can't believe this is happening," she said, shaking her head.

She buried her head in her hands then looked up at Cory. "Oh, my. Now that I recall, I think he did have a bit of an accent. This is truly incredible!"

Cory thought the poor woman had enough badgering. Besides they should be hungry by now. The rain had stopped. Cory offered to go around the corner to a nearby take-away as the Brits called it, but Allison preferred to eat out because she didn't want to be alone awaiting Cory's return.

They hadn't heard from Ben, but Cory reasoned he was too busy. Allison didn't expect to hear from the party whose number Hamid had provided and he had her mobile number.

Allison led the way. Linking arms with Cory, she walked briskly and hummed Paul Simon's tune, "Feeling Groovy."

Cory kept silent puzzling over Allison's sudden animation. Plagued by depression since adolescence, Allison reported occasional relief with brief spurts of energy which appeared close to manic in intensity. Her mood swings made her a good candidate for lithium.

An enigma, she could fit the picture of a substance abuser, but that was unlikely since she was too smart to lug that stuff through customs, and her physician had said she was averse to drugs. Could she have gone out earlier for a brew or two? It was doubtful. Cory wanted to discuss her condition with Betty, but the time zone difference and Betty's hectic schedule made it difficult to fit in a consult. Nevertheless, she planned to try after Allison went to bed.

A study in contrasts, Allison shifted from eating binges followed by vomiting, to fasting. She was smart, savvy and sophisticated, yet at times acted emotionally immature.

Hamid, her husband was another riddle. A devoted family man, he was involved with a mysterious woman. An Iranian, an informant for the C.I.A., he was a petroleum engineer for a multinational company that would profit big time from an environmentally safe way to reinvigorate non-producing oil wells.

"This must be the place I read about in the guidebook," Allison said, halting at the entrance of a restaurant. Cory pushed through the door surprised by the elegance of the ornate Victorian furniture and well-dressed patrons.

The host ushered them to a corner table exquisitely laid with fine china. A Tiffany lamp shed a warm glow over the creamy beige lace tablecloth. Allison took her time studying the contents of the gilt edged, blue velvet covered menu. Cory figured she was counting each calorie of every dish. Finally, she made a choice. "Parchment wrapped Scottish salmon," she said to the tuxedo-clad server.

"Make that two, please," Cory said.

Allison fingered the tableware. "Good quality. And that lamp! I wouldn't expect to see it here." She continued to focus on the decor until the meal arrived. Allison dug in with gusto leading Cory to wonder if she'd keep it down.

"This is healthy, low calorie stuff. I promise not to—you know," she said as if she'd read Cory's mind.

Cory smiled, digging the fork into a moist sweet potato. Apart from the hum of conversation from nearby tables, they ate in silence. Although they had been in London less than a week, it felt like an unending odyssey.

The main course over, the server brought a dessert tray. Cory's frustration made her crave sweets. She pointed to the succulent looking pear tart. "Would you like to share it with me, Allison?"

"Absolutely not. I know when I've had enough," she said over the rim of her teacup. Was she chiding Cory?

Again, as if she knew what Cory had been thinking, she said, "Go ahead, Cory. You probably need the energy. You know, for some reason which I don't understand, I'm suddenly optimistic."

"Perhaps you're encouraged because we may have a handle on your situation. Also, now that the agency's aware of it, they should be able to help."

"I pray Ben will soon find my family." She checked her watch. "It's hard to wait to hear from him. Should we call?"

"No. He's probably turned off his mobile to avoid calling attention to himself." Cory wondered if he'd eaten.

Allison slipped her credit card from her purse and reached for the bill.

Cory placed her hand over Allison's. "Please let me take care of it this time."

"Absolutely not. You're here as my guest."

"At least let me pay the tip."

She shook her head. "It's included in the bill."

"You're very generous, Allison, but it's not necessary for you to pick up my food tabs. I chose to be here because I care about you. I enjoy my independence and want to pay my share."

"I'm sorry, Cory. I truly hope I haven't offended you. I did what I thought was appropriate. Next time we'll split it. Okay?"

Cory nodded. "I know you meant well, Allison."

There were aspects to this woman Cory really liked. She was generous, had social grace, and apart from her eating disorder, reasonable. They walked out of the restaurant on to the quiet street, arm in arm, and a spring to each step, with the warmth of two friends.

As they strolled along the avenue, two black bearded swarthy men, their dark eyes blazing, yelling in an unfamiliar tongue, stormed toward them. Allison froze in her path.

Cory grabbed her hand. "Let's get out of here. Run back to the corner."

Heavy footsteps pounded the pavement behind them. Cory glanced over her shoulder. The men were catching up to them. As the light turned red, they raced across the street leaving the men on the curb facing the traffic. Cory pulled Allison into the shelter of a crowded hotel lobby.

"What was that all about? Why were they after us?" she asked, breathlessly, clutching her chest.

"Frankly, I think we aborted a pick-up." Cory giggled. "To those guys, two unescorted women seemed like an invitation. We were spooked over your situation that's why it scared us."

Allison rolled her eyes.

Cautiously glancing behind, they left the hotel from a rear door that led to their street.

When they opened the door, Allison glanced at the wall clock. "Ben should have called by now," she said, biting her lower lip.

"I know, but worrying won't help. Ben knows what he's doing. He's probably too involved to phone." Cory's counsel was directed to herself, too. "Let's watch the news."

Allison carried the portable TV into the sitting room and set it on a small table.

"They call this silly thing a telly, here." She plugged it on and surfed the channels, repeatedly returning to a sitcom on BBC. "Nothing," she said, furrowing her brow.

"Maybe news is broadcast on the hour. Let's try then. Meanwhile that show could distract us."

Allison's face reddened. "Do what you damn please!" she yelled, storming into her bedroom.

Her mood swings were hard to tolerate, but under the circumstances, she was entitled. Afraid she'd prematurely rid herself of the meal she'd consumed, Cory chased after her. "Anyone would be frustrated in your situation," she said.

Allison turned to face her. "Oh Cory! I'm truly sorry for my outburst, but I feel so helpless. I don't know what to do?" She wrung her hands. "I'm anxious to hear from Ben. I want my family back," she sobbed.

"Let's go into the kitchen. Maybe there'll be news on the radio and we'll find out there's been a power outage or a traffic problem."

They tried several stations that carried local news, weather and traffic conditions, none of which interested them. The time passed slowly and Cory's concern for Ben's safety grew. Finally, she grabbed the phone. "I'll call him now." She punched in the numbers and let it ring several times. "No answer. Maybe I hit a wrong button." She tried again with the same result. She was tempted to call the police, but what could she say? As she pondered this quandary, she had a graphic image of Ben in a pool of his own blood.

"It's after ten o'clock and still no word. There's no use waiting up, Allison. You may as well go to bed and try to get some sleep." Cory covered a yawn. "I'll be on the phone for a bit attending to my office affairs. If you need me, please knock on my door."

"I understand, Cory. How selfish of me! I forgot that I'm not your only patient."

"Not a problem. I've got good back-up."

Cory needed privacy to call Betty. She longed to hear her voice, to feel comforted by her and to get her slant on the current patient. "Goodnight, Allison." Cory closed her bedroom door. When she heard the water run in Allison's bathroom, she punched in Betty's number and was delighted that she picked up the phone.

"Hey Cory. How's it going?"

"Not so well. There are big problems here. I'd like your professional opinion."

"Sure, but before you start, let me tell you about the weird call you received two days ago from Ingrid Gunderson."

"Ingrid? Really! Remember I told you about her—the abused woman I befriended on the plane going to San Francisco who seemed to have vanished."

"Well, she resurfaced. She's safely ensconced in Canada and wants very much to speak with you.. Wait. Let me get my glasses on." She paused. "Okay, ready." Betty read the number Ingrid had left as Cory copied it. "When I picked up your call, she was reluctant to talk to me, but after I assured her you wouldn't allow anyone but a trusted colleague and confidante to take your calls, she opened up and said to tell you she hired a private investigator to tail Mohammed who was tailing you. This sounds like the Farmer in the Dell, Cory."

"I wish it were that simple. I don't know what to do about it. I wish Ben were here. He's been out since this morning looking for kidnapped kids and a possible abduction of their father. He hasn't checked in with us and it's awfully late here. I'm worried."

"Geez, you sure have an exciting life, Cory."

"Oh yeah. Remind me not to complain about the monotony of San Diego ever again!"

"It doesn't have to be dull. I'm having a ball."

"Who is it this time, Betty?"

"A Charger quarterback."

"Go on!"

"Gotcha! "

Next door the water stopped running. Cory snapped on the radio and tuned it to a soft pitch.

"Ah, yes!" Betty continued. "Getting back to my notes, Mohammed skipped the country for the U.K. The detective Ingrid hired wants to hear from Ben. He left his number. Ready?"

"Uh-huh," Cory copied the number.

"Hey, the next part is kind of jumbled—I wrote this very fast, Cory. I'm sorry. Let's see—she said she sent you warning notes."

"Ah-ha! One part of the riddle is solved. Thank you."

"Warning notes? Don't keep me in suspense. I'm dying to hear all about it."

Cory gave her partial information, leaving out the dangerous stuff.

"It's hard to believe. My friend, the therapist and part-time private eye. What intrigue! You must keep me posted. This is like a soup opera."

"Soup?"

"Yes. A pea-soup opera. Murky. Now didn't you want my opinion on something?"

They discussed Allison's psychological condition for the better part of an hour. Betty supported Cory's efforts and reaffirmed the difficulty treating eating disorders. Cory recited her address and phone numbers in London and they signed off. Cory's head whirled as she put the pieces of the puzzle together.

If her suspicions were correct, Mosen who assumed the name Mohammed was sent to familiarize himself with Hamid's surroundings. Noticing Cory's daily visits to Allison, he had spied on her to find out who she was and what she was doing there.

Frightened of Mohammed, Ingrid had hired a private investigator to tail him. When she learned Mohammed was shadowing Cory, she kept her distance, but slipped her the warning notes. As Cory had tried to protect Ingrid, Ingrid had tried to protect Cory.

She examined Ingrid's phone number and figured the time difference was either six or nine hours behind London.. She checked her Timex and became more alarmed. It was nearly eleven o'clock and no word from Ben. She phoned Ingrid, but there was no answer.

Convinced Mohammed and Mosen were one and the same, she had to know who employed him and for what purpose. Another oil conglomerate who wanted Hamid's technological information? Was it an ally or an enemy of the United States?

Maybe Mo's mission was to dispose of his cousin and take his engineering post. Was he really a rival or posing as one to protect Hamid. Allison suggested there was a strong family allegiance. After all these years without family contact, would his allegiance remain?

Cory crawled into bed and lay there puzzling and sleepless for an hour. She heard the doorknob rattle.

=29=

"You look like you've just seen a ghost!" Ben said, quietly closing the bedroom door behind him.

"You frightened me. We were worried because you didn't call or answer your phone."

Moonlight shone on his grimy, lined face, making him appear ten years older than when she had last seen him. "Oh, Ben, you look awfully weary."

"I am very tired. A lot happened," he said, sitting on the edge of the bed. "Before I crawl in, I better clean up." He pulled off his rumpled jacket and shirt and tossed them on the chair.

"Shall I make something for you to eat?" Cory asked, rolling off the bed.

"Don't fuss. Toast and tea will be fine."

"You got it."

Cory tiptoed to the kitchen, heated the kettle and toasted slices of Hovis bread. She was happy that he was back, but anxious about the news he would soon reveal.

She rummaged through the fridge and pulled out some cheese, a ripe tomato and mustard.

By the time the table was set and the tea and sandwich were ready, Ben stood in the doorway clad in gray sweats and socks, his dark hair damp and his face freshly scrubbed.

Resting her elbows on the table, Cory waited patiently until he scarfed half of his cheese sandwich. "Okay, tell me already."

"It's been quite a harrowing night. I had to call in M.I. 5—that's British Military Intelligence. You see, I tailed the guy we think is Hamid's imposter to a remote abandoned brewery far from Prupetrol. Anyway, I peeked into the windows. You won't guess what I witnessed." He bit into the rest of the sandwich and slowly chewed.

"Are you deliberately dragging this out to hold my interest?"

Ben nodded and sipped the tea. "I caught sight of a bunch of guys—no doubt terrorists, busily assembling plastic explosives."

"What? You're sure?"

"Come on, Cory. Of course I'm sure. I know how explosives are made. I saw them molding the stuff on the work table in front of them. I notified M.I. 5 and they dispatched a bomb squad team."

"My oh my. I'm sorry, Ben. I feel stupid having asked a thoughtless question."

"Listen, Cory. You're not stupid. You're half asleep. I'm sorry to put you through all this worry. Anyway when the good guys arrived, the bad guys must have heard the cars outside because they abandoned their gear, hurried away and made their escape through a tunnel. They were prepared for a get-away."

"And then what happened?"

"The bomb squad went inside and disassembled the stuff."

"Where were you when that went on?"

"Listen, Cory. I don't take chances. Obviously I was a safe distance away. You see, I made it here okay." He stood and twirled around surprising her with his agile clowning.

"Did they catch them? Do they know who they are?"

He shook his head. "Not yet, but they will. They won't get too far. The crime scene folks got perfectly fresh fingerprints and DNA. But that's not all. We suspect the hideaway may have been used for the production and storage of other mighty lethal stuff."

"What?"

"Remember I told you they were working out of a brewery? Well, it's pretty easy to produce biological agents such as plague or anthrax, and just as easy to conceal them in an abandoned brewery as in a pharmaceutical plant."

"Shocking! Terrifying!" The chilling possibilities made her shiver. Noticing it, he rose from his chair to wrap his arms around her, but his gesture afforded small comfort. "Did they find anything else?"

"I hope not, but I don't know. I wasn't going to hang around."

"Thank God you're here." She hugged him tightly. "How would they attack with those weapons?"

"Probably with artillery, or missiles. Maybe aircraft mounted with spraying tanks. Aerosol canisters could be sprayed in crowded places or on food supplies."

"Food supplies?"

"Unfortunately, it's possible."

Cory's head pound. "I've read about the international ban on such weapons."

"Big joke! There really aren't any strong enforcement provisions."

"You're kidding! What good is the ban? To give people a false sense of security?"

He shrugged, returned to his seat and finished his sandwich.

"Ben, this is horrible."

"It appears that hostile nations haven't yet perfected a long range delivery system to strike us, but it's conceivable that they'd use the technology on their neighbors. It's bad, but the effects are treatable if diagnosed and treated fast."

"But are we prepared for such a strike?"

"Well, the Pentagon is doing a good job with research and measures for protection. Better than FEMA, the Center for Disease Control and the FBI. Take heart, Cory, no reports about such incidents have occurred in the states. Some big cities are already prepared for biological terrorism."

The subject made her queasy. She sipped peppermint tea. "You're saying that we really aren't adequately prepared."

"Three senators have applied pressure. Let's hope it ignites the others."

"Only three? Such apathy," Cory said, rinsing the dishes and stacking them in the dishwasher. "That reminds me, talking about biological weapons. Wait till you hear what Allison has told me."

She quickly filled him in.

"No doubt Mosen is Hamid's imposter. I watched him engineer the making of the explosives. I'm pretty sure he's the leader of those young terrorists."

"I wonder why he's involved, Ben. He's not from a fundamentalist background."

"You're the psychologist, Cory. Work on a theory."

Next, she told him about Ingrid's call and handed him her detective's name and phone number. Then she supplied the good news phone message from the recording interpreter.

Ben glanced at the wall clock. "It's four in the afternoon there so I ought to reach these guys now. I'll catch you in bed."

"You've got a date," Cory said, stifling a yawn. "But a tired one." She padded to the bedroom leaving Ben in the kitchen.

Anthrax, plague, food supplies, good grief! Cory vowed to do something about that when she returned to the states. Chilled, she climbed into bed and pulled the warm, soft peach colored covers up to her chin. She wanted to hear what Ben learned from Ingrid's detective, but her eyelids grew heavy. She closed her eyes and drifted asleep.

≈30≈

Awakened by the aroma of coffee, Cory turned and reached for Ben. His side of the bed was warm, but empty. She pulled on a pair of jeans and a tee shirt, brushed her teeth and hurried to the kitchen where she was surprised to find Ben and Allison laughing.

"Good morning. What's so funny?"

"Ben just mentioned a sign he saw in a London office." She filled Cory's cup with freshly brewed coffee, presented a pitcher of cream and a plate of toast

Cory inhaled the familiar scent and sipped. "Mmm. Delicious."

"After tea break, staff should empty the teapot and stand upside down on the draining board," said Ben.

Cory sputtered and grabbed a napkin. "That is funny."

"They have a way with language," Ben said. "How about 'Toilet out of order. Please use floor below.'"

"It's a good thing there's no food in my mouth," Cory said, enjoying the much needed levity.

"Hey, ladies, how about a jog after breakfast?" Ben asked.

Allison declined, but told them to go ahead. She said she felt more secure now that Ben was back.

Cory tied the laces of her running shoes, pulled on a hooded sweatshirt and off they went into the chilly morning fog.

"What did you learn from your calls last night?" Cory asked, stuffing her cold hands into her pockets.

"The phone messages were reconstructed with the help of a Farsi interpreter. Curt, business-like conversation between Hamid and a woman. It was devoid of affection. The sole purpose of the calls was to make several noon lunch dates."

"Hmm. Maybe Hamid could be some kind of double agent," Cory whispered.

"I don't know, Cory."

To keep warm, they sprinted to the park. By the time they arrived, the sun broke through the mist casting lemony rays. The thick carpet of grass appeared light green and the leaves on the trees shone silver. Joggers and cyclists traversed the edges of the path while women pushed prams in the center.

"This seems such a peaceful, safe place. So orderly. It's hard to imagine how the kids were snatched here. Are we any closer to finding them?"

"Sure hope so, Cory."

Lost in an image of Allison smiling and hugging her children in a family reunion, Cory felt a smile form on her face.

"There's more news," Ben said, interrupting her fantasy.

"What? From Ingrid's detective?"

"Yeah. The guy's an old buddy of mine. He found out that Mohammed is suspected as the leader of a small group of terrorists. An offshoot of Hamas, according to the CIA,"

Footfalls from a runner approached them from the rear. They stopped talking and glanced around. The man huffed past them. Another jogger was a reasonable distance away.

"And obviously from what I witnessed, it's true. Believe it or not, this klutzy guy has a reputation for being elusive."

"He wasn't very effective as a snoop in San Francisco."

Ben nodded. "Both the CIA and M.I 5 now know he's an impostor working at Pru-petrol. They're aware of the kidnapping and that Hamid may be held hostage."

"Hey, wait a minute, Ben. If Mohammed fled when M.I.5 showed up, do you think he'd be back at Pru-petrol today?"

"Good question. That's the first place they'd look. I was certain his only role was to learn Hamid's process, but when I saw him assemble the explosives... Anyway, once he's apprehended, I'll be notified."

Cory tugged at Ben's elbow. "Let's slow down, I'm out of breath."

He accommodated his pace to a brisk walk.

"Maybe Mo wears two hats, Ben, a political terrorist and an industrial spy."

"Those roles can overlap. Mo, Mosen, Mohammed, a Christian who aids Muslim terrorists? What's his motivation? I understand spying for money, but what does he gain from his deadly business? The CIA doesn't seem to know any more about him than we do."

"I don't think monetary reward is his only motivation. It's revenge. Allison said Mosen has always been jealous of Hamid. The terrorist stuff may be a macho thing. Some people try to compensate for what they perceive as their weakness by flexing muscles. Mosen assumed an Arab name, got involved with these young bandits and became their leader."

Ben stopped to tie his shoelace. "Interesting. Cousins Mosen and Hamid each play two roles--maybe."

"Have you notified anyone about the phone message records?"

"Yeah, I'm waiting for a call-back. I may meet someone this morning. We're not in this alone, Cory, but we can't wait for the big guys to do our job."

"Did Hamid and this woman ... what is her name?"

"Shadi."

"Did Shadi, the shady lady and Hamid have a special meeting place?"

He chuckled. "Yeah, they lunched at the White Castle in Bloomsbury."

"Hah, a relative of the old hamburger joint in New York?"

"Hardly, it's an expensive restaurant."

"Well, then, should we make a reservation there for lunch today?"

"No. I don't have time. Now don't you dare check it out on your own. It's too dangerous. Hang around with Allison and don't take her anywhere near that place. Someone may recognize her."

"Let me offer a hypothetical, Ben. Supposing this was a case of industrial espionage, not political terrorism. Wouldn't it be possible for me to dine at the restaurant, pull out Hamid's photo and ask the waiter if he remembered him and his female companion."

"You're sure this is hypothetical, Cory?"

"Absolutely."

"Why would the waiter respond?"

"I'd say I'm a friend of the family and we're worried because the man on the photo has disappeared."

"Listen, Cory, many people don't want to get involved."

"You're right. I'd lay some cash on the table. You know. A hint-- payment for information. Anyway, the photo is of Hamid and the children. That could make a difference. Never can tell what might turn up."

"And if he had no information?"

"I'd beg the waiter to ask the staff and I'd speak to the host to see if anyone overheard anything that could lead us to Hamid."

Ben halted, stepped in front of her blocking her path. "Don't you dare do it!" he shouted. "I forbid it!"

Her face flushed. "I beg your pardon."

He touched her shoulder. "I'm sorry," he said, gently. "That was paternalistic. But it's for your own good."

"Haven't I proven to you that I can take care of myself? Remember when we were hijacked and I foiled that creep?"

"True, but this is different."

"Both are life threatening situations."

"Come on, Cory. You can't compare the two."

"Okay. Let's drop it. What have you told Allison?"

They resumed walking. "Well, she knows about my adventure yesterday and that British Military Intelligence and the CIA are working together to locate Mohammed. She figures when that happens, we'll find Hamid and the kids and everyone will live happily ever after."

Cory sighed. "Allison's entitled to know about the Iranian woman."

"Yeah, she'll need your help with that one."

"I'm puzzled. Allison knew Hamid had government connections. Doesn't she suspect that Hamid wasn't just an informant—that he could be an agent and perhaps a double agent?" Cory asked.

"She could be more concerned that her husband has ditched her for another woman. Double trouble."

"I doubt she'll believe that. Especially after you explain the recorded conversation was business-like. Besides, she's convinced he loves her."

He shot her a seductive glance—for the moment warming her all over, until she remembered his macho outburst.

"Listen, Cory. I've good news about Ingrid. When my old buddy heard that her husband is a UN diplomat and a friend of Mohammed, he reported it to top level security people. Now, should it be proven that Ibrahim is connected to a terrorist, he'd be ruined. And Ingrid would be safe from him."

"That's great! I tried phoning her last night, but there was no answer. I can hardly wait to speak to her."

The mobile phone rang and Ben took his call. It was clear from his conversation that he would have an early appointment.

They ran back to the flat. Cory looked for Allison, but she was gone. Her note on the kitchen table stated she went off to order items for Mattingly Manor from a specialty store and would return after lunch.

Ben was about to leave when he turned to face her. "Listen, Cory, "Don't wander off on your own. It's much too dangerous."

"I heard you the first time, Dad. Now, will you please stop this harangue?"

He shook his head and closed the door behind him.

When she was sure he'd gone, she snatched Allison's family photo from her room and reached for the phone. She had to help find the children.

⸗31⸗

For a premium price, the clerk at the photo shop invited her to wait while he reproduced Allison's family photo. She looked around. Posted on the walls were several glamour shots of Princess Diana with the studio's name embossed.

Duly impressed, when the technician handed her an exact copy of Allison's treasured photo, she said, "Thanks for your fine work."

Cory rushed back to the flat, replaced Allison's possession, and grabbed a taxi to the restaurant in time for her noon reservation.

She stepped into the carpeted, softly lit, windowless dining room. A glance at the wide expanse between tables led her to understand why Hamid and Shadi had chosen White Castle for their clandestine rendezvous.

The host seated Cory at a corner table facing an oil portrait of a handsome man; her make-believe lunch companion. Judging by the subject's clothing, the fine work of art was painted in the nineteenth century and appeared museum quality. She hoped she had enough cash to pay for lunch and a bribe.

The waiter, a tall, lean, middle-aged dark complexioned man, presented a menu filled with exotic choices. Cory chose the lowest priced item, a Greek salad and refused his wine suggestion. He scribbled the order on his pad and dashed away.

Cory dug into her purse, pulled out the photo of Allison and her family, and studied it again. Hamid, a handsome man with warm brown eyes under thick dark eyebrows, had a large dark mustache that framed a pleasant smile. The children had the same coloring as their father. Allison gazed lovingly at the cherubic baby seated on her lap.

Awaiting the server's return, Cory tapped her fingertips on the water glass, and scanned the room. She saw the waiter scurry from table to table engaging in animated conversation with patrons with whom he appeared familiar. It was obvious the White Castle catered to a crowd of regulars. Cory figured that was a good sign.

Finally he headed for the kitchen and returned with a large platter. With a flourish, he slid the dish on her table. "Enjoy, madam," he said, peering at the photo.

"Excuse me," she said, pointing to Hamid's picture. "Does this man look familiar?"

He hesitated, his eyes widening as though in recognition. "Why do you ask?"

"He and a female companion lunched here often, and now he's disappeared."

The server flushed. "That is most unfortunate. I do beg your pardon, madam, but who are you and why do you ask me?"

"I'm a family friend. I was hoping perhaps you'd overheard something that could lead me to him."

"Many people dine here. I don't remember every customer."

"They were regulars... I'd hoped... well, perhaps if you'd show this photo to the staff." She shoved the money toward him. "I'd gladly pay for your trouble."

"Madame, I am very sorry, but we're very busy, now," he paused as she gave him a rehearsed sorrowful look. "Perhaps you'll come back after the lunch crowd."

"Yes. I understand. When would be a good time?"

"Two-thirty."

"Thank you," she said, digging into the crisp salad. She lingered over lunch, ordered coffee and sipped slowly. Over the rim of her cup, she saw her server stand at a table in the rear of the room pointing in her direction. She began to have second thoughts about the merits of her investigation, but tried to ignore them.

She sashayed toward the restroom clutching her purse and attempted to sling it over her shoulder when she approached the spot where the waiter had pointed at her. The table was occupied by two businessmen types one of whom looked vaguely familiar, but she couldn't place him. Engrossed in conversation that sounded like Farsi, they didn't seem to notice her. Cory figured London was home to many nationalities, nevertheless it was a coincidence.

Her makeup kit rolled out spilling its contents near their table. She stooped to retrieve the fallen objects and to eavesdrop. One of the men kneeled down to help her. She thanked him. He smiled at her and continued conversing with his companion in English.

After paying the bill, she pocketed a White Castle matchbook, whipped out *The London Guide* and decided to explore the nearby semi-residential district in the time remaining before her planned return to the restaurant.

Cory passed several elegant 17th and 18th century squares and headed up Gower Street to University College. Founded in 1826, it was the first British college to admit Jews and Roman Catholics. The structure reminded her of a building at the City University of New York campus where she was proud to have attended graduate school. City had strict academic standards, high quality faculty and remarkably low tuition.

Behind the college at Gordon Square, she spent time examining the facades of restored 19th century town homes one of which housed a collection of Chinese ceramics from the 10th to the 19th century. Admission was free. She tried to enter, but a posted sign said it was closed during lunch.

Continuing her history trip, she poked her head into the Dickens Museum—the house where Charles Dickens completed *Pickwick Papers* and *Oliver Twist* and was now filled with memorabilia from his early life. She figured an overview of the area was all time permitted, but vowed to return for a thorough look around.

Beneath an ominous sky she high-tailed it back toward White Castle and arrived at the precise moment of a downpour.

The waiter greeted her, locked the door and rolled down the window shades. Immediately her stomach sank and she felt overwhelming dread—a horrible trapped feeling, as when alone in a disabled elevator in an empty building.

She told herself it was probably customary to draw the shades when a restaurant closed. Nevertheless she couldn't shake her fear. "Someone will be meeting me here momentarily," she said. "On second thought, I should wait for him outside."

He shook his head. "Not in the rain, madam." Be assured, we'll open for him when he comes. Please follow me to the office. We have a lead for you."

He escorted her to the rear of the room, opened a door and shoved her in. The door lock snapped.

=32=

Cory found herself in an enormous office facing a large, heavy set man who stood before her wearing a shaggy sweater, a garlic scent and a face in need of a shave.

"Not to worry, lady. You answer questions and I will not hurt you," he said gruffly.

She twisted the doorknob, but as expected, it was locked from the outside.

"Why have you trapped me in here? I've done nothing wrong." She glanced around the room, noticed several doors and tried to figure out where they led.

"You ask too many questions of waiter," he said. "We want to know why you look for this man?"

"I'm a friend of his wife. We came from the states to see him, but when we arrived, he had disappeared. We understood he lunched here with a woman associate."

"How do you know this?" he asked, hoarsely.

"He mentioned it to his wife."

The gruff man shook his head. "I not think so."

"How else could we have found out?"

"That is what I want to know." He clenched his fists and moved toward Cory, his eyes narrowing. "You tell me who else knows about the missing man or I wring your neck."

Cory hesitated. "Let me see. I'm trying to remember if there's something my friend said that I may have forgotten."

He leered at her.

"Look. If you'd stop trying to frighten me, I could think better." He backed off.

There were three doors in the room. The one leading back to the restaurant was locked. The other doors could possibly lead to her escape.

"Well?"

"There's nothing else I can offer. I don't know of anyone who is interested in him, except you."

"Why does your friend not look?"

"She's sick and distraught. She's worried that he may have run off with the woman."

He laughed so hard, his belly shook. "I think you lie and I do not like that. I like better to make you scream until you say the truth."

Cory fought off her terror with anger and glared back at him. He inched toward her with his jaw clenched and his hands aimed at her throat, but she had a surprise for him.

"KIAH!" she yelled, turning to the side. She raised her leg and kicked him hard in his stomach.

Eyes bulging, he gasped, fell forward, striking his head on the sharp edge of the desk. He grunted and crashed to the floor.

She scurried across the room toward a door and flung it open. Damn! A closet.

She dashed to another door at the far end of the room, pulled it ajar and found herself outside in a rain soaked narrow lane.

Her pulse racing, she sloshed through puddles, splashing muddy water all over herself--a small price for freedom.

At the end of the passage was the familiar square she had explored earlier. She breathed a relieved sigh as though she had come home. Several black cabs lined the street, she headed toward them, but other dampened pedestrians beat her to it.

At the curbside, she hailed a passing taxi, but it didn't stop. A black car rolled to the curb. The driver leaned forward and opened the door. "No," she said, shaking her head. Two men came from behind and shoved her into the backseat. They piled in beside her and slammed the door.

"What the devil!" she shouted. She turned and saw the two Farsi speaking diners from White Castle.

⸗33⸗

The shorter of the two men spoke softly to the driver who nodded, lowered his gray tweed cap over his brow and shifted into gear.

"Did you really think we would allow you to escape?" The taller man said, his rough jacket sleeve brushing against her cheek as he tied a blindfold across her eyes.

"Why are you doing this to me?" she asked, trying to stop her teeth from chattering.

"We need to know your involvement with the Iranian gentleman about whom you have made inquiries." Her captor spoke low and his breath smelled of tobacco. She concentrated on his voice. It was unfamiliar, but his face hadn't been. She couldn't figure out where she had seen him before the restaurant.

"All you have to do is ask and I'll tell you, instead of scaring the living daylights out of me with these tactics."

"My regrets. Now we must take you to a quiet place where we will be sure of your cooperation in privacy."

Cory shrugged off a chill and tried to stop imagining what they had in store for her. Although she had heard him speak Farsi, he appeared to be British educated. She judged him and his associate to be somewhere in their forties. Earlier, she had noticed they were immaculately groomed and expensively clad businessmen types. "Suits," as one of her patients would say. Now, closely sandwiched between the two, she caught a whiff of fragrance and focused on the scent, certain it was Paco Rabanne X-S.

"Look, I've never even met my friend's husband. She wanted company on her trip to London and asked me along. The only thing I know about him is that he's an engineer."

"I think you know much more than that," he said in a solemn voice like that of an undertaker.

"But I don't. Really. Why do you want to know about him? Who are you?"

"I am sorry, but we are not at liberty to explain."

"How long do you expect to hold me?" she shouted.

"That all depends."

"On what?"

Ignoring her, he spoke to his colleague in Farsi.

"My friends expect me back soon. They know where I lunched today. When I don't show, they'll notify the authorities of my absence."

"No one will recall your visit. Your friends will think something prevented you from reaching the restaurant."

"Oh, no they won't. You see, when I phoned from the White Castle, I mentioned where I was calling from," she said, regretting that she hadn't really done so.

"Nevertheless, nothing will come of it. You are a foreigner."

"I am an American citizen. We have an embassy here."

"Do you really think that matters?" he said, chuckling.

She figured he needed to scare her, but then again, it was possible he had an ally at the American Embassy. "What do you plan to do with me?"

"We have ways to make you talk, he whispered. When we are satisfied, we will drive you to a taxi stand."

"But I don't know anything more than what I've told you and your henchman at the restaurant."

"So you say now. By the way, how did you manage to knock him out?"

"What? You think I did it? He tripped and fell. How is he?"

"When we left him, he was unconscious."

She wondered how soon he'd be able to tell them she was responsible. Her stomach lurched as she contemplated how they would torture her, or kill her. She should have listened to Ben. What a fool she was, out of her element.

When she failed to make an appearance at the flat, Ben would figure she had gone to White Castle, but how would he trace her from there? And if he could, would it be too late?

As she tried to figure out an escape plan, her palms grew damp. In a deliberate display of nervousness, she clutched her purse on her lap and groped for the mobile. If she fingered the right button and spoke loudly, perhaps her voice would penetrate the leather. Then she remembered the phone would beep. It would be reassuring to lay her hands on it. At least there'd be a tinge of hope, of possibility for later. She continued to knead the purse, but couldn't feel the instrument. Of all the luck! It must have rolled out with her makeup kit.

"Damn!" she shouted "What a way to spend my vacation!"

"I am sorry this has turned out so badly for you."

Yeah, I bet you are, she said to herself

She listened for street sounds—some evidence of the area they traveled, but it was quiet, apart from the rumble over cobblestones.

About five minutes later, the vibration stopped and the drive increased speed as they drove across a smooth surface. Overhead, she heard geese cackling. For the moment, a comforting pastoral sound.

The men spoke rapidly to each other. From their conversation, she understood the taller man was called Kami and the shorter, Bahran. She wondered where she had heard Kami's name before, but she couldn't remember.

The trip seemed endless and it was hard to judge the time or distance. She had visions of arriving at a deserted farmhouse where her screams wouldn't be overheard by neighbors. Perhaps it would be the place where Hamid and the children were held hostage, too.

The car slowed, bumped along on what seemed to be a long gravel driveway and then stopped. She was nauseated with fear. Kami removed the blindfold and helped her out of the car. A real gentleman.

They stood at the entrance of what looked like an abandoned warehouse. The front windows were boarded up. She scanned the blighted, deserted area and concluded there was nowhere to run. The driver rolled down the window and muttered something that sounded like he was going for petrol. He made a U-turn and pulled away. The car evaporated in a cloud of dust and flying pebbles.

Cory had a karate move in mind to foil the men as they escorted her toward the rear of the building, but figured it was too risky. Although they hadn't shown a weapon when they captured her, she was afraid they could be armed.

Kami jiggled a key into a rusty padlock and it flipped open. He thrust his fist against the warped door. The hinges squeaked as he held it ajar for them. A concrete stairway led to lower and upper levels. Bahran climbed the stairs. "Please follow him," Kami said as he filed behind her.

They reached the top of the flight and stepped into the corridor. Bahran unlocked a door and they followed him into a huge room painted sunny yellow. He turned around and mumbled something about going out to wait for the car. She heard his heavy footsteps as he clambered down the stairs.

"A kindergarten!" she said, noticing colored blocks of various sizes and shapes that lined the perimeter of a blue plastic playhouse. A sandbox containing pails and shovels sat in the middle of the room and assorted toys and stuffed animals lay on a low shelf.

"Please sit down and relax a moment," Kami said, pointing to a low couch placed against a wall next to a bridge table and chairs. "Something to eat or drink?" he asked, moving toward a squat refrigerator on top of which sat a microwave oven.

"Just some bottled water, if you have, please." She planted herself on the couch and looked around. In the far corner was two pair of bunk beds placed kitty-corner in makeshift dormitory style. An open portal revealed a stall shower and lavatory.

Kami handed Cory a cold bottle of water and a paper cup.

With shaky hands, she poured water into the container and sipped. "Looks like all the comforts of home are here. Where are the children?"

"I assure you they are well and happy." He cranked the handle of a small casement window emitting fresh air and the sweet sound of children's voices. "Come, have a look."

She stood at the window overlooking a courtyard and saw a little girl and a young woman rolling a small red ball back and forth to each other. Nearby, a little boy was trying to jump rope. A tired looking man guarded them from his perch on a rickety looking wooden chair, a newspaper on his lap.

"Is the woman their regular nanny?"

"Yes. As you see, we have done all we can to make everyone comfortable here. We have no harmful intentions providing there is cooperation."

Abduction was pretty darn harmful, Cory thought, but was in no position to argue the point. "I wish I could help, but I don't know how," she said.

"Sit down at the table. Slowly remove your identification and hand it over to me."

Carefully, Cory rooted through her large purse and felt the outline of the phone that she had stashed in a zippered compartment. Reassured, she withdrew her wallet and began to thumb through it for her I.D.

"No. Give that to me." He held out his hand. A dark red mark covered the bottom of his right thumb. His fingernails were manicured and lacquered to a shine. On his shirt cuff were the black embroidered letters KK

Kami pulled out a small leather bound memo pad from the inside pocket of his jacket. He tugged and twisted a slip of paper stuffed in her wallet. Unfolding it, he read off the address and phone numbers of the London flat. "That's Hamid's place, isn't it?"

"That's where we were headed when we arrived in London, but he wasn't there."

"And these phone numbers?"

"Don't remember."

"Really? Where are you staying?"

"The Wellington" she said.

After scrawling on his pad, he studied the identification on her driver license and copied it. "Cory Cohen of Del Mar, California." He examined the next document.

"And this one states you are a psychologist," he said, holding up to the light, the cheap bit of pale green paper that was her psychology license. "California must not think well of your profession judging from the flimsy certificate."

"The government likes to save money. At least patients value me."

"Really? Well, I daresay this is bogus. No doubt it is your cover."

"What? Check it out with the Psychology Board."

"Either you are impersonating the real Cory Cohen, or your documents were fraudulently manufactured. Now, tell me who you are working for."

Cory's fear quickly turned to frustration. "Myself. I'm in private practice. Call my office. What do I have to do to prove I'm telling the truth?"

Hands clasped behind his back, Kami began to pace. "In due time you will have your chance."

She wondered what prospect lay before her.

"How do you know Hamid's wife?" he asked.

"She hired me because she was emotionally distraught over the separation from her family."

"Ah, yes. You are supposed to be a psychologist."

162

She gulped the water and it went down the wrong way. After a brief coughing spasm, she cleared her throat.

"How do you know Hamid?" he asked.

"I've never met him," she said, hoarsely.

"Speak up! What do you know about him?"

"Just that he's an engineer on a project here."

"What kind of project?" Kami asked, hovering over her.

"Allison never mentioned it, nor have I asked. It wasn't relevant."

"Why do you think he has disappeared?"

"Well, at first because Allison and Hamid were estranged, we thought he was involved with another woman, but now I see what you're driving at. It must have something to do with his work." As soon as she said that, she realized why Kami's face and name were familiar. His photo appeared in Pru-petrol's annual report. This man, an abductor, was a member of the Board of Directors!

"My company has paid Hamid handsomely for developing an advanced methodology which would give us a tremendous advantage over our competitors. He has promised it to us. Only to us. But he has not delivered. Until he does, you and the children shall remain here. Without her husband and children and her supposed psychologist, his fragile wife will have no emotional support. That should make Hamid rush to meet his commitment." Although his reasoning was otherwise flawed, Kami seemed confident of Hamid's devotion to Allison.

"Look. If Hamid hasn't come through to release his children, my being here isn't going to make a bit of difference."

"No doubt you are right, but we can't dismiss you quite yet."

"Why, not? I've told you all I know."

"If you yourself are not directly involved in obtaining Hamid's process, I believe you are aware of others who are."

"That's impossible. I don't even know what it is for." She paused. "Is it something to prevent wrinkles, I hope?"

His jaw clenched. "I don't appreciate your sarcasm, Doctor Cohen—if that's really your name."

"I'm sorry if I offended you, but I was serious. There's plenty of money to be made in cosmetic engineering."

Kami stared at her. "Others are eager for what he's developed. Very eager. We think he has promised it to them, too. We must know! We must be absolutely certain no one else obtains it." He shook his finger at her.

"You've piqued my curiosity. What has he invented?"

Kami's face darkened. Despite the unusual circumstances that had brought them together, he had been civil and polite, but now enraged, his eyes blazed. "Your cocky attitude, this self-assurance will be diminished quite soon, Doctor Cohen."

"Look. You've taken me, an innocent person hostage in the hope I can give you information which I don't have. And to boot, you think I'm an imposter. How do you expect me to react?"

"Cooperative and yes, I suppose angry and frightened."

"Maybe what you see as my bravado is a cover-up for fear."

"Now you sound like a real psychologist, Doctor Cohen."

"Thank you, but it isn't effective in gaining my release. By the way, where is Hamid?"

"At his place of business."

"Wait a minute. Isn't he your hostage?"

"Yes, in a manner of speaking. He's free to come and go to work. He knows if he makes one false move—well, we have his children."

Of course! Mo couldn't go back to Pru-petrol. They had to send Hamid. She began to see Kami the big shot for what he probably was. An industrial spy.

"How often do the children see their father?" she asked.

"Daily. He lives here."

"Then I'll meet him tonight."

"I do not think so. You will be out like a light by the time he arrives."

"You mean he'll be here late?"

"No. I must give you an injection now to make you talk."

She knew Sodium Pentothal had been tried as a truth serum, but was now considered ineffective. Cory was terrified about the drug contained in the injection.

She squeezed her eyes shut to summon courage and strength. Her head whirled. She hadn't earned a black belt for nothing. Perhaps if she took on the men by surprise one at a time, she could prevail. Now, she was alone with Kami and she had no idea when Bahran would return, she must act fast.

Kami opened the refrigerator door and pulled out a small cardboard box. He carefully peeled off the seal and removed a syringe. Approaching her, he squirted a drop of liquid. He was ready to inject.

Her heart pound so loudly that she thought he could hear it. "What—what is that?" she asked, trembling.

"This is a new solution developed by one of our scientists. A truth serum designed to replace sodium pentothal."

"I'm allergic to drugs. Damn it! I could die," she shouted, knowing full well, he couldn't care less. No doubt this man had tried to have her killed in San Francisco and was responsible for the murder of Allison's chauffeur.

"We shall soon find out," he said, leering.

She moved away. "No. Please. You'll gain nothing from this."

He took another step toward her, his right thumb poised on the syringe, ready to plunge.

"Don't hurt me." She held up her arm to show cooperation, but when he came close, she turned, catching him off balance. She wrenched his right hand with hers and twisted his wrist. Startled, he struggled to release her grip and accidentally plunged the syringe into his thigh. "Eee," he screamed, his eyes rolling back.

Grabbing her purse, she dashed out, scaled the flight of stairs and tugged open the rickety door to the front of the building. She scrambled down the gravel driveway onto a deserted road.

She pulled out the mobile, punched 999 and asked the dispatcher to track her and send help.

"Sorry Madam. We do not have the capability to detect the location of calls made from mobile phones"

"Look. I've just escaped from two men who brought me to an abandoned warehouse about an hour or less from Gordon Square. Please have someone find me before they do. I've no place to hide. Question the waiter at... " Damn! The light on the mobile went off. It had lost power.

Cory figured the man who had dropped them off at the warehouse had driven off to buy gas, so the station might not be far away. Racing along the path she surveyed the area in vain.

She ran and ran until her chest burned. Finally, she stopped to catch her breath.

Hearing a vehicle approach, she scampered into the tall weeds at the side of the path where there was a decrepit wooden crate. She crouched behind it. As the car passed, she peeked out and saw Bahran and the driver. Headed away from the warehouse, they could be on their way to collect Hamid at Pru-petrol. That meant she would have time to disable the guard before they returned.

She raced back toward the warehouse plotting an escape with the nanny and kids.

She would need to create a diversion in order to overpower the men and snatch the car keys. The plan was risky, but she had no choice.

≈34≈

Breathlessly, she arrived back at the warehouse and after fumbling around, finally found her way toward the courtyard entrance. Constructed in an old fashioned style similar to the Brooklyn school buildings of her youth, the top half of the door had a thick glass window. She ducked down and cautiously raised her head to eye level. Miraculously, the guard appeared to be dozing. She slid out into the courtyard. The nanny saw her and gasped. With her finger on her lips, Cory motioned to her to keep silent and mouthed the words, "We must escape."

She grabbed the children's hands and came toward Cory. The guard snored and the children giggled. "Hand me the rope and ball and give me your scarf, Molly," Cory whispered.

"Okay," she answered. The children hid behind her. "It's quite all right. We are going to have fun playing a game with our new playmate," she told them.

"Now hurry inside and wait in the corridor," Cory said.

Molly and the children did as asked.

Cory's hands tingled as she measured the length of rope against the task ahead. Barely adequate to tie the guard to the chair, it would make a harness if woven between his outstretched legs. She tiptoed behind him. As she started the job, he awoke and tried to fight her off, but his seated position rendered him vulnerable. He thrashed about, kicked and tried to tip the chair backward, but Cory held it firm and he couldn't reach her. Swiftly, Cory stuffed the ball into his mouth securing it with Molly's scarf. She tightened the rope with knots remembered from a sailing class.

Rushing into the corridor, she bent down to speak to the children. "I'm Mommy's friend. Here, look at this." She pulled out the photo of Allison's family. "See. Here's Mommy, Daddy, and you two. We're going to see Mommy today. She's waiting for us at the apartment where you lived with your daddy."

"Won't that be nice," Molly said. "We'll have a party, just as we've pretended."

"Mommy! Oh, my Mommy!" the little girl cried, clutching the photo to her chest.

"I'm a big boy. I don't cry," Allison's son said.

"Now, now. It's fine to cry. Especially for joy," Molly said, combing his hair with her fingers. He wiped his tears with the back of his hands.

Despite what she'd been through, surprisingly, Molly appeared to trust Cory. Perhaps because Cory was female. Anyway, she had little alternative. Cory explained her plan.

They hid behind the gate to the driveway, and played games. Her rule required that the first person to hear an oncoming car must sing a song.

"You remember the one I taught you this morning, don't you?" Molly asked. They smiled and nodded.

"Then we must be very quiet to listen," the boy said. "That's boring!"

"We can play quietly and still have fun. Remember Charades?" said Molly. An excellent Nanny, she found ways to hold the children's interest and time passed without incident.

As a car approached the lane leading to the warehouse, the children sang, "Mary had a little lamb."

"Bingo!" Cory called, running out the rickety gate.

At the far end of the driveway, she whipped out the White Castle matchbook pocketed earlier, struck several matches and tossed them into a dried bush. A small fire started. Quickly, it began to blaze. Her heart crashed against her chest, fearful that they may not escape in time. She raced behind a large rusty trash can at the opposite side of the driveway.

In the seconds it took for the car to arrive, the fire had spread to the adjoining brush, away from the warehouse structure. Bahran and the driver jumped out of the car leaving the doors open and the motor running. They raced into the building, presumably to fetch a fire extinguisher or a hose. Cory slid into the car and drove toward Molly. She ran to the car with the children in her arms. Face glistening with sweat, she plopped into the backseat of the car and slammed the doors. They sped away.

"Do you know how to get to the flat from here?" Cory asked.

"It's a bit difficult, but I shall do my best."

"Just get us to civilization, Molly. A service station can't be far off."

"What? Oh, you mean petrol. Yes. It's just before you reach the motorway."

Initially, the children probably had thought this an adventure, now they seemed to pick up on Cory's anxiety and started to cry. Molly tried to soothe them. This tender young woman deserved honors in child care.

"Look, there's a phone here," she said.

"Call 999, Molly. Tell the dispatcher to have someone collect those thugs—if they can find them. One may be unconscious, upstairs." Cory gave her the *shpiel* about the restaurant and asked her to repeat it to the police.

She did as asked, adding a request for the Fire Brigade. "The fire may not have been contained," she said and proceeded to give them an approximate location of the warehouse. When she terminated her call, Cory gave her Allison's number. Molly spoke softly to her and then handed Cory the phone.

"She's quite hysterical. She thinks this is a ruse."

Cory pulled the car to the side of the road to talk on the phone, interrupting Allison's sobs. "Look, Allison. We've made our escape and the kids are fine. Please calm yourself because they're eager to talk to you."

Molly gave each child a chance to speak, then handed the mobile back to Cory.

"I'm driving the kidnapper's car and going directly to you. I'll ask Molly how long it'll take."

"Under an hour, but to be sure, tell her longer," Molly whispered.

"We should arrive in about an hour or so. Please tell Ben about all this, now."

Following Molly's instructions, after forty minutes, they arrived.

"Surprise!" Cory shouted, flinging the apartment door ajar.

Allison ran to them. "What? Oh, my Lord! I can't believe it, truly" Her smiling face flushed, she opened her arms. "Mommy, Mommy," the children cried as she scooped them up, hugged both tightly, and smothered their cheeks with kisses.

"Let's go into the kitchen," Cory said to Molly. They went into the kitchen and Cory poured orange juice which they promptly gulped down and refilled their glasses. She stared at Cory.

"You are an incredible person."

"So are you, Molly McBride."

"I don't even know your name."

"I'm Cory Cohen. I came here to help find you and the kids."

"That is precisely what I thought when I first saw you. The other day, in secret, Mr. Meckenian told me his wife had hired a detective. You are she, then?"

Me, a real detective, Cory thought, nodding, her mind drifting to Ben.

"Excuse me a moment." She picked up the kitchen telephone and punched in his mobile number. Ben answered immediately, gasping when he heard her voice. "Cory, where the devil are you? I've been worried sick. All Allison told me was…"

"I'm fine and man, do I have a lot to tell you."

"I bet you do. I don't know how you pulled it off. You sure are something else!"

"I'm beginning to believe it."

"Listen, there's a foul up with Hamid. M.I.5 picked him up at Pru-petrol. They're convinced he's Mohammed!"

⸗35⸗

"That's easy enough to disprove, Ben. Come collect Allison. She'll be thrilled to make an identification."

"Quit anticipating my moves, Cory."

"Sorry. Look, I can use a big hug from you."

"And I need an explanation from you."

"Sure, Dad. How soon you coming over?

"Twenty minutes or so. And enough with this Dad stuff. Listen, Cory. You'll be asked to scrutinize a lineup at the police precinct today. I don't want the apartment unattended. I've hired a big, blond muscle man, Sven from International Security Services. He should be there any minute. He'll have a badge." Cory shuddered, hoping Sven's presence would be for naught.

Peeking into Allison's open bedroom door, with joyful tears Cory watched her comb her daughter's hair, clipping it back with the child's pink barrette she'd found when they had first arrived. The little girl, eyes closed, sat on her mother's lap and seemed to be dozing off, perhaps tired from the excitement. The boy lay on the bed, his thumb in his mouth.

"Sorry to disturb you, Allison," Cory whispered. "Ben's on his way here to pick you up. Seems MI 5 is interrogating Hamid. Unfortunately, they're convinced he's Mohammed. You're needed to identify your husband."

"Oh my Lord, what if the man isn't Hamid?"

"That's unlikely. The kidnappers told me he was at Pru-petrol today and that's where MI 5 found him."

" But…oh, I must fix myself up. I haven't seen him in such a long time." She gently laid her sleeping daughter on the bed and covered the children with blankets.

Cory slipped out of the room and into the kitchen where Molly busied herself tidying up. Looking out the window, she realized the sun had set and the sky was darkening.

The doorbell rang. Through the peephole she spied a huge blond, smiling man. He held up a badge. "Sven from International Security Services," he said.

Cory let him in, introduced herself and Molly. Setting eyes on this Adonis, Molly blushed. He was far more attractive than the tired guard at the warehouse.

The strain of the day began to take its toll on Cory. She yearned for a few peaceful, quiet hours to call her own—to recuperate from the trauma of her adventure.

When she heard a rap on the door, she knew it was not to be.

She squinted through the peephole and saw two uniformed officers. "Police. Open up," the woman officer said, harshly.

"I had no intention of doing otherwise," she said, unlocking the door. "Please come in. It's admirable how quickly you responded."

"Are you the woman who was abducted?"

"Yes, I'm Cory Cohen."

"We're here to escort you to the station to identify the suspects," the officer said, flashing her ID and badge.

"Fine. You should know they've committed a graver offense— kidnapping children and holding their nanny hostage. Won't you need her as a witness, too?"

"Yes. Of course," the policewoman said. "I'll notify the Yard. They handle kidnapping."

"This presents a bit of a problem," Molly said. "The little ones are sleeping now and I can't very well leave them."

"Understood. Someone will come for you later. Under no circumstance, must you leave the area."

Molly nodded. It was certain she preferred staying with the children.

"Wait a second. I have something that will identify one of the men," Cory said. The officers followed her into the bedroom and watched her rummaging through the dresser drawer. She located the Pru-petrol Annual Report and tucked the thick document under her arm before heading downstairs and into their car. Off they went to the station house.

A solemn duo, the officers made no conversation. Cory tried to engage them in a friendly exchange about the similarities of police work in their respective countries, but they seemed to prefer a silent ride, leaving Cory to rest quietly. Finally they pulled into a parking space adjacent to a police station, much like many others she had seen on BBC TV productions.

The officers seated her at a conference table opposite two plainclothesmen and then disappeared. To her right, a glass, fashioned as a window on her side and presumably a mirror on the opposite, faced a brightly lit room into which she expected would soon hold a lineup.

The detective inspectors spoke their names, titles, date and time into a recording device and examined Cory's I.D. before questioning her.

About a quarter of an hour later, the interview was interrupted when ten men began to file into the room on the other side of the glass, each holding a numbered placard. The man who had driven her to the warehouse held up the number four. Bahran held six, and the guard, eight. Kami wasn't present.

If the syringe, meant for her, held a lethal substance, it was unfortunate for him that he'd accidentally injected himself. Her act of self-defense was designed to escape from him. Subsequent events weren't her responsibility, but would anyone believe her?

"There was another man. Kami. What happened to him?"

"We had the warehouse searched. There were only three men."

"Bahran, that's number six. He and Kami were the men my waiter had pointed me out to at the White Castle restaurant. By now you must know there's something fishy at that place. And I don't mean the food."

"Yes. The dispatcher has explained about the restaurant. We've sent someone to investigate."

"And?"

The inspectors ignored my question.

"Something must have happened to this Kami. Wait a sec, please," Cory said, thumbing through Pru-petrol's Annual Report. "Look. Here's a photo of him. Kami Khatami, Ph.D. This is the man who abducted me. Can you believe that he's Vice President of Research and Development?"

"Are you absolutely certain it's the same person?"

"Two men named Kami who look exactly alike are both involved in oil? I'm almost positive."

"Almost, huh?" He turned to his associate. "Make an enlarged copy of this photo and have it sent at once to the Yard."

"What did he want of you?" the detective asked.

"He was sure that I worked for a rival company. He pressured me for proprietary information, which of course I didn't have. He said my I.D. was a forgery and I was an imposter, pretending to be a psychologist to Hamid's wife—that's the man whose work his company coveted. As you know, the couple's kidnapped children were held in that warehouse, too."

From the frozen expression on the inspector's face, Cory figured he interpreted her babble as that of an incomprehensible hysteric which at that moment wouldn't be a great reach.

"Hamid?"

"Hamid Mekenian, a petroleum engineer. The husband of the woman I escorted to London in search of her kidnapped children. He had refused to have Scotland Yard on the case and feared the consequences of a big splash in the newspapers," Cory said.

"That's not unusual in a kidnapping case, Doctor Cohen. I assure you, we are not offended."

"I suggest you contact Detective Johns of the San Francisco Police. This situation is tied to his investigation. Doctor Kami Khatami may be a suspect in a murder and conspiracy case."

The detective stared at her.

"It's true. I wonder how Doctor K. got away today, especially—"

"Yes?"

Cory explained the syringe incident. A look of disbelief flashed across the detective's face.

"Truth is—"

"Yes. I know. Truth is stranger than fiction, " he said, finishing her sentence. "While it does appear odd, I have no reason to doubt you. I've checked on your credentials. Your prints are on file with California and match those collected at the warehouse."

"Yes. Back home, fingerprints are required of all licensed psychologists."

He smiled as though he understood her defensiveness. "We may need more information from you at a later date. If you plan to travel, do check with us first." He handed her his card. "Someone will drive you back, now."

Cory rose to leave. The detective inspectors thanked her for her cooperation and escorted her to the reception area where she was met by two uniformed officers who drove her back. Another tight-lipped ride.

When she reached the flat, the children were asleep on Allison's bed and Molly curled up on the living room couch with her eyes closed. Cory tiptoed into her bedroom and plopped into bed.

Too excited to fall into the deep stupor, she had expected, she tossed and turned, reviewed the events of the day and had a hard time putting it to rest.

What the devil happened to Kami Khatami? How could he have escaped? Perhaps the effects of the injection were brief, he recovered quickly and someone picked him up before the police arrived. Or ... he could be lying dead, his body stuffed some place the police hadn't searched. In the absence of Doctor K's remains, the detective had no reason to arrest Cory. Even if the man had died, she was not responsible.

Surely the detectives wondered, as did she, why a high ranking official of a large corporation would take charge of her abduction.

That Kami Khatami had suspected her of being an imposter although he hadn't a shred of evidence, led her to the conclusion that he was paranoid. Lacking trust in others, he took on critical jobs himself. Perhaps there really were no rival companies privy to the fact that Hamid was on the brink of a revolutionary technology, and this was all part of Doctor K's paranoid delusion.

Voices in the corridor interrupted her musings. Eager to meet Hamid, she hopped off the bed, slipped into clothes and hurried into the living room. But it was not to be.

⚮36⚮

"Where's Hamid?" Cory asked, plopping down on the sofa next to Molly.

Allison and Ben had parked themselves on the living room chairs and discrete Sven had slipped into the kitchen.

"Being grilled at MI 5," Ben said. They took a long time checking Allison's documents. Put her over the coals, too." He smiled at Allison. "You're a good trooper."

"A careful lot they are," Molly said.

"Too careful, if you ask me," Allison said, massaging her forehead. "I've got a whale of a headache."

Molly pushed herself off the sofa. "A nice cuppa, then. Would you like an aspirin?"

Allison shook her head. "No thanks, but tea would be fine. I'll go check on the children."

Once they were alone, Ben and Cory fell into a hasty, all too brief, tight embrace. "Cory, you had me worried. You took a hell of a chance."

"Yeah, but it paid off. I wish you'd have more confidence in me. What's their reason for holding Hamid?"

"They want more information about his cousin. He tried calling Mosen's parents, but couldn't reach them. MI 5 wants to make sure he phones in their presence."

"Makes sense."

"At first Hamid thought it was ridiculous that Mosen changed his name to Mohammed. He refused to believe a guy he regarded as a brother would impersonate him, but when presented with evidence, he became furious. Betrayal is hard to take. I should know."

She stroked his back, recalling what Ben had said about his former wife, a woman who had rejected both him and their kids for her law professor. Only mothers with serious attachment issues could give up custody of their children for the sake of fulfilling their selfish dreams. "Have you found out anything about Shadi?"

"Not yet. If I hadn't reported that terrorist activity to MI 5, they wouldn't have given me the time of day."

"Come on, Ben. It's your charm."

"Can it help me get you on a slow boat to China—like right now?"—

She was about to show him how much she would appreciate that trip, when Molly entered the room followed by Sven carrying a tray with steaming teacups.

"The kids are fast asleep," Allison said, returning. She reached for a cup with her shaky hands. Liquid sloshed on the saucer.

Sven jumped up. "Sorry. I must have overfilled." He handed her a napkin.

Allison smiled at him. "I'm glad you've joined us. It truly makes me feel safer. But Cory and Ben, now that your job is done, you aren't going to leave me, are you?"

"Not until things have settled," Ben replied.

"I can't ever thank you enough, Cory. You've put yourself in danger for my children. How can I repay you?"

"From time to time, remind me that you enjoy a healthy, happy life. That's the best reward."

Ben stood and stretched his arms above his large frame. "I'm ready to pick up some chow for us. How's the all night take-away, folks?"

"Sure. I'm glad you didn't suggest the White Castle," Cory mumbled.

"Excuse me, I'll rest until you're back," Allison said, her hand on her forehead.

As Cory and Ben trooped down the street, she had a creepy feeling that they were being followed, but when she glanced over her shoulder, no one was there. Ben wrapped his arm around her. "The night air is chilling," he said. "And you're hungry and tired."

They ducked into the tiny take-away and stood at the end of a short line which soon grew. Cory remained with a peculiar sensation that someone at the rear was up to no-good. Raising the collar of her raincoat, she huddled next to Ben. He gave their order and they waited at the cash register to pay. Cory scanned the faces of the people on line. All appeared innocent. Drumming her fingers on the counter, she attributed her anxiety to her recent experience— a bit of post-traumatic stress. That she had prevailed was a near miracle.

A little later, they marched into the quiet flat. Ben plunked the large sack on the table and Molly started opening the vaporous containers of spice scented food. Sven brought over disposable plates and utensils. While Molly dished out portions, Cory went to check on Allison.

She lay on the bed, a wash cloth over her eyes.

"How are you?" Cory whispered.

"Happy, but scared for Hamid."

"I understand. Come join us for a bite, please. He'll be here soon."

"Oh! I'd like him to catch me eating," she said, sliding off the bed.

Midway through their meal, the doorbell rang. Sven went off to check and Allison traipsed behind him.

"I think it's your husband," he said from the hallway.

Allison dashed to the door and flung it open. "Hamid. Hamid!" Allison shouted. A moment later, he followed her into the kitchen. Cory's mouth flew open as she stared at the man, the spitting image of the omnipresent imposter.

~37~

Could Allison be wrong? Was he really Hamid? But MI 5 had let him go. His resemblance to the man they had seen in San Francisco was startling. Recalling the voice and accent of that guy, Cory longed to hear this one speak, but all he did was nod at Allison's introductions.

"You've had quite an ordeal. Please join us," Cory said, making room for him at the table.

"That's true! I'm hungry, but I'll pop in to see the children first." Much to Cory's relief, his accent bore only a slight trace of the Middle-East. But then again, Mo could have feigned poor English.

Cory glanced at Molly. She seemed to sense Cory's thoughts. "They're fine and fast asleep. Oh, Mr. Mekenian, it's unlike you to wear the clothes you wore to work at dinner. Dear me! Everything is at the warehouse."

"Not so, Molly, I've brought it all here, in the foyer. It's—one of the reasons I'm so late. Some men from Scotland Yard had to photograph the crime scene and they took me back there." He looked longingly at our half-eaten dinners and parked himself next to his wife.

Molly filled his plate and he wolfed down the food. "Now to get cleaned up," he said, pushing himself away from the table. "Then off to bed with my dear family at last!" He sighed.

"I think we're all ready to hit the sack," Cory said, tossing the used paper plates in the trash.

Sven carried his sleeping bag into the kitchen and Molly made up the couch.

Finally alone, Ben and Cory made the most of it, despite exhaustion. Despite expecting a reprimand for her activities, she detailed the events of her day. Perhaps Ben figured the means justified the end because in place of a lecture was his obvious delight at her presence.

In the morning, they awoke to the fragrance of breakfast in progress. "Mm, coffee and something vanilla," Cory said. Hurriedly, they got ready and tiptoed to the kitchen. Passing

Allison's bedroom door, they overheard the delicious sound of laughter. Cory smiled at Ben and he squeezed her hand.

Sven, his broad back to them, was whipping up a batch of pancakes while Molly transferred the finished products into a warm oven. Their efficient assembly line gave hope that Sven could help dissipate the horrors of Molly's past ordeal.

Appetizing aromas and children's laughter transformed the ambiance of the flat. The place was no longer grim. With Allison's family reunited, the job was almost done. Tying up a loose thread, like Kami Khatami, who had a few loose threads of his own, and then Ben and Cory should be on their way. Shadi remained on Cory's mind, but she wasn't their job. Nor was Mohammed aka Mosen.

Cory admired Ben's ability to finagle his way with the authorities, and when he picked up a call for from a cordial man from MI 5, it didn't surprise her. "You have an incredible way of making friends with these guys, Ben."

"Well, I'm on their team. They asked me to drive Hamid there, now."

"Look, Ben. This crowded apartment is giving me claustrophobia. Drop me off at a department store. I'll do some shopping while Sven's on watch here."

"Sorry. I don't want you out alone."

"I'll be fine in a busy store, Dad. I promise to taxi right back."

They argued until she won.

Cory passed the perfume counters, bereft of patrons, and strolled toward the umbrellas where there was a deep discount sale. She elbowed her way through the crowd, smiling over the ironic line she'd given Ben about claustrophobia.

Suddenly, a familiar scent intruded. Paco Rabbane X-S. She stopped in her tracks and like a bloodhound, turned and sniffed around, but couldn't pinpoint it. Her palms grew damp and her stomach, queasy. She had to get out of there.

Rushing toward a salesperson, she requested the restroom. She was directed to an alcove a few yards away and raced toward it. To her dismay, there was an entrance fee. She fished around her in purse, but didn't have the correct change. That did it. She wouldn't shop in such an inhospitable place. She flew out the door and hailed a taxi back to Kensington.

Ben and Hamid returned later in the day. Handkerchief in his hand, Hamid dabbed at his reddened eyes, staggered into his bedroom and closed the door.

"What's wrong?" she asked Ben.

"Let's go for a walk." He slipped her raincoat off the hook and handed it to her. "We won't go far," he said grabbing an umbrella, but we may get caught in a downpour."

"Back soon," she called, trooping behind Ben.

When they reached the pavement, Ben faced her and took her hands in his. "Listen. Yesterday, MI 5 asked me to hide Hamid's mobile so he couldn't use it while we slept."

"They're still unsure of him?"

"Investigators never accept things at face value. Anyway, Hamid just spoke with his aunt and uncle—Mosen's parents in Jordan. He couldn't reach them yesterday because the family was attending a funeral." He paused. "Hamid's parents were killed in an automobile accident."

"Oh my God!"

"He thinks Shadi's behind it. She had threatened to have his parents killed if he didn't hand over his process. A hell of a choice—his parents or his children!"

Cory heard a distant rumble of thunder, but Ben continued.

"Hamid told everyone that his system had some bugs and he needed time to fix it. Actually, he deliberately sabotaged his work. What else could he do? He was between a rock and a hard place." Ben wrapped his arm around her shoulders. "Now he feels responsible for the death of his parents."

Ignoring the black streaked, pewter sky, they started toward the park. "But maybe it really was an accident," Cory said.

"His aunt and uncle hired an investigator."

"They suspect foul play?"

"Hamid told them he'd been threatened."

Cory stooped to tie her shoelace. "What about Mosen?"

"His parents said he's working for some French company. They haven't heard from him in weeks."

Far away, a few gold rays poked through the dismal sky. The optimist inside her thought maybe it wouldn't rain, after all.

"Naturally, Hamid's broken up. Looks to me he can profit from counseling. Grief and guilt. A double whammy." He shook his head. "Maybe he'll be your new patient."

Cory shrugged. "Allison and the children will console him. I'll let him know I'm available."

"Good. Listen. He suspects Shadi works for a company that leases wells in Iran. Did you know that country produces half the amount of oil today as it did in 1973? They need a hefty boost. Figured Hamid was their ticket."

"This is too complicated. I'm glad it's not our business. What bugs me is Doctor Kami Khatami's whereabouts. Yesterday, I asked the police to notify Detective Johns because Doctor K may be a suspect in a murder investigation in San Francisco."

"Yeah, I know you did. I've spoken to the detective who interviewed you. The men you identified accepted a plea in an exchange for information. Bahran said he'd found Kami having a seizure. At the time you'd thought they were heading to Pru-petrol to collect Hamid, they were actually taking Kami to a private hospital."

"Must be I didn't notice him because he was stretched out on the backseat. Have the police got him?"

"No. The doc released him this morning."

"He must have given his address."

"Yeah. The Wellington Hotel."

Cory shivered. "Oh no!"

"What's wrong, Cory?"

"I told him I was staying there."

"Interesting. I didn't take you for a liar."

"That's not funny, Ben. Damn! For sure, he'll try to come after me."

"Take it easy, Cory. Scotland Yard's looking for him and his photo is plastered in every law enforcement agency here and abroad. It won't take long before he's apprehended."

"That's comforting. I wonder who'll be found first, Mohammed, Doctor K. or Jimmy Hoffa."

Large raindrops splashed the ground. "We'd better head back," Ben said, opening the umbrella. She slipped her hand through the crook of his arm.

"Listen, Cory. Doctor Khatami's on an extended leave from Pru-petrol. He was on the way out and desperate."

"No surprise."

"And that waiter of yours—well, he's related to the owners of White Castle. They're wealthy Iranians. Live at a villa in Cannes. They're Shadi's friends."

"It had occurred to me that the waiter was Kami's pal. I wonder if he knew that two of his customers were rivals for Hamid's process," Cory said.

"Strange that Kami didn't know of Shadi and Hamid's rendezvous there. They must have come at different times."

"Maybe she's sunning herself on the French Riviera, now."

In the distance, a bolt of lightning crashed. "This wasn't a good time for a walk in the park," she said harshly, rushing to keep pace with Ben.

"Is there any point in my warning you not to go off on your own until that man's apprehended, Cory?"

"You have a funny way of stating what you think you shouldn't," she said, angrily. "Look. Expect my rotten mood to hang around, until Doctor K's locked behind bars."

"Listen, Cory. You can choose to blame me for the mess you're in because I initiated it, but take into account that you were warned not to go on your own to White Castle."

Her face grew hot. "Look. If it weren't for me, the kids wouldn't be with Allison now."

"Maybe or maybe not. You've got to stop jumping into things without considering the possible consequences."

She sighed. "You're right. For years, Grandma had tried to drum it in, too, and do you know I convey the same message to impulsive patients? What a hypocrite I am!" She wondered what more she would need for the lesson to sink in.

⸗38⸗

Molly and Sven had prepared dinner. Allison came to the table with the children and announced that Hamid just learned his parents were killed in an accident. Hamid, head bowed, sat down next to his wife.

"Oh, dear," Molly gasped. "I'm very sorry for your loss, Mr. Mekenian."

"Thank you," he said staring at his plate.

"Please eat something, Hamid," Allison said, softly. "You need strength."

"I lost my mother last year. We expected it because she'd been sick for a long time," Sven said. "It was still hard. But an accident? The shock—that's tough."

"It may help to talk about it, Hamid," Cory said.

He raised his head. "I appreciate everyone's kindness. Please go about your business. I'll be okay."

Allison tried to cheer her husband. "Take a look, Hamid. I've eaten everything on my plate."

He gave her a faint smile and poked his mashed potato with a fork.

The somber evening ended early with everyone hitting the sack.

The next day, Hamid's grief coupled with Cory's apprehension began to change the atmosphere of the Kensington flat and affected the children. They became cranky, whined and cried easily despite Molly's Herculean efforts to distract and humor them. Blessed with patience and common sense, she remained at her post, but the trauma had begun to take its toll. Sapped of energy, Molly muttered to Sven, rolling her eyes frequently. Cory figured that if it weren't for her loyalty to the children and her obvious attraction to Sven, she'd resign.

Ben's business took him away. Sven tried to engage Hamid in a chess game while Molly, Allison and the children made cookies. They invited Cory to join them, but she didn't want to crowd the kitchen. Left alone, she craved a run in the park, but the darkening clouds looked ominous and she didn't want to be out by myself.

Soon the rain splattered the windowpane. Trapped, Cory needed a distraction. It was a decent time to call overseas. She thumbed through her notebook and found Ingrid's phone number that Betty had provided. "*Bon Jour*," said a cheery voice on the other end.

"Ingrid?"

"*Cest moi*," she replied.

"It's Cory Cohen."

"Cory? How wonderful to hear from you. Where are you?"

"Stuck in dreary London on a case. What's going on with you?"

"I suppose the British press hasn't reported my good news."

"I don't read North American society pages, Ingrid."

"Very humorous. That asshole husband of mine has been stripped of diplomatic immunity. I wish they'd strip him of his balls, too. Anyway, because of his association with terrorists, he's being deported. The weirdo who tailed you in San Francisco— Mohammed Daqamseh—well, he was picked up with Ibrahim at our flat."

Chilled by the turn of events, Cory was eager to share it with Ben. "How did you find out?"

"It was in *The New York Times*, yesterday. Page two."

"I'm sure glad to hear it. What will you do, now?"

"I think I'll stay in Canada for a bit, until I'm sure he's out of the U.S. When are you returning to the states?"

"Soon, I hope."

"Keep in touch, Cory. Give my regards to that big man of yours. And thanks so much for being my friend when I really needed one."

She phoned Ben and shared the news.

"Incredible. Here I sit at MI 5 and they've no idea that Mohammed was apprehended in New York. Who is holding him?"

"Sorry. I should have asked, but I was so eager to tell you, I goofed."

"Don't worry about it. We'll get on it now. This means we could be out of here soon."

"Aw shucks! I was beginning to like this gloomy atmosphere. Oh! Should I tell Hamid?"

"Let's wait until we have all the facts. "I've got to go. We'll talk soon."

"You think there could be some mistake?" The line was dead.

⸗39⸗

Sven's attempt to pull Hamid out of the doldrums worked. Deep in concentration, the two men sat opposite each other focusing on a chessboard. Sven, his chin cupped in his hand, and Hamid, furrowed brow weaving his thick dark eyebrows into a distinctive singular line. "Checkmate," Hamid announced, placing his knight in position.

Sven studied the board and shook his head. "Good game!" he said, leaning back on his chair.

"Do you play Backgammon?" Hamid asked.

"Sure."

After Hamid won again, Sven went into the kitchen to help Molly prepare for dinner.

"How well do you know Kami Khatami?" Cory asked Hamid.

"He was my main contact at Pru-petrol last year, but this time 'round, he was on an extended leave of absence. A rumor spread that his divorce caused a decline in his mental health. He had refused a generous settlement package in exchange for his resignation.

"Khatami was determined to prove his worth by claiming my work as his own. After the children were kidnapped and he abducted me, I realized the extent of his pathology."

"Did you report him?"

"I couldn't. He threatened to hurt my children if I did."

"Why is your work so important to him?"

"Khatami is a brilliant man. Known for being on the cutting edge of new scientific findings, but he's nuts—uh—forgive me please—mentally unbalanced." Hamid smiled sheepishly. "If he claimed my work as his, and took it to a rival petroleum company, he'd be back in business."

"Perhaps Doctor K.'s emotional disturbance pushed his wife to leave," Cory suggested.

Hamid shrugged. "I quite understand Khatami's humiliation. He'd been loyal to a barren wife who divorced him. Such things are shameful in his culture. We weren't close, but he told me his family warned him not to marry an English woman. Now, all he has left is his work."

"And no scruples," Cory said.

"True. I'm sorry, I've been so upset over this whole business, plus the loss of my parents, I haven't thanked you properly for all your help."

"You've just done it." Cory smiled. "Do you have any idea where Doctor K could be now?"

"He knows many important people here. He could be hiding out at someone's country estate."

"Do you think he's a vindictive person?"

"Perhaps. I'm no psychologist. And he's changed since I first met him. I never would have expected him to do all this dirty work, but many people manage to hide their darker side."

"I suppose that goes for your cousin, too."

"I've been thinking about that. Mosen was always a bit odd. Out of tune. Some years ago, he fell in love with a very young girl, his best friend's sister from a fundamentalist Muslim family. It didn't sit well with his Christian parents or with hers." Hamid folded his hands. "He said the relationship had ended, but he could have lied. Perhaps he converted, took a new name and married her."

"We've got cracked Doctor K. on one side, and your imposter cousin, another oddball on the other."

Hamid chuckled. "It's funny, the way you put it."

"Some folks have a preconceived notion of how psychologists speak. They may expect formality. Maybe my style convinced Khatami that I wasn't a real shrink."

"That's entirely possible."

"In your opinion, would he be prone to strike back at me for escaping with the kids?"

"It's difficult to say. Everything he's done has been motivated by his desire to obtain my work. Not long ago, he employed a woman engineer to seduce me to work for her company on a secret project. She offered a huge salary, bonus and extra perks—such as sexual favors. She invited me many times to the White Castle restaurant in an effort to seduce me with promises of a fortune and with her body. I wasn't interested. I trapped her into admitting her connection with Kami Khatami.

"Was this woman named Shadi."

"Yes."

"Do you know her whereabouts? Cory asked."

"No, but I must warn you. Khatami is very suspicious and he may try to hurt anyone connected to me. He may have harmed Shadi because she knew too much and failed in her mission to seduce me. You must leave immediately. You've done a superb job and needn't stay any longer."

"I may be needed as a witness. I'd better ask Ben."

The front door swung open. "Speak of the devil," she said as Ben sailed in.

He hung his damp raincoat on a hook in the hallway and pulled out a folded newspaper from his attaché case. He spread the paper on the table. "Here, read this."

They pored over the report of Mohammed's capture by the FBI in New York. A photo of him appeared next to a photo of Ingrid's husband. Mohammed was a dead ringer for Hamid.

Cory figured Mohammed aka Mosen must have worn several hats. He may have forced Middle Eastern café owners to contribute to a terrorism cause.

"It's verified. We're free to leave now," Ben said.

"Won't they need me at a trial?"

"Under the circumstances, your signed statements will do. I'll make travel arrangements."

"I should call my aunt and uncle," Hamid said. "I hate to give them more bad news. My parents, and now this."

Allison grasped his hand. "Perhaps it can wait until we're back in California."

"It will be hard for me to speak with them no matter where I am. Perhaps it will be better for them if they hear it from someone else."

He glanced at Molly. "I can finish my work from home. After what has happened, perhaps you'd like to reconsider your agreement to work for us in the states."

"Well, I'm very attached to the children, but safety is a concern and I've heard about crime in America. It does sound a bit frightening."

"Would you feel safer if we hired a body guard, like Sven?" Hamid asked.

"Heavens! I'd feel like a royal." She blushed.

Allison turned toward Sven. "You're a big comfort. Truly. With our chauffeur gone, we'll need a replacement."

"I've never been to the states. It sounds appealing, but I'll need a contract and a work permit."

"Let's talk about it. I know someone who can expedite the paperwork," Hamid said.

"About your chauffer, do you have any idea why he was killed?" Cory asked.

"Yes. One evening Klaus came to me and said that Doctor Khatami had contacted him and wanted him to spy on me, to see if he could find any notes I brought home from work. Klaus said he seemed desperate and frightening. Klaus was very loyal. He'd been with Allison's family for a long time. He was much more to us than a chauffeur. He was like one of the family."

Allison started to sob. "I knew him all my life. He was like a live-in-uncle. We depended on him for so much."

"I know how much Klaus meant to you, Allison. He was very protective of the household—a talented handy-man around the house and the Bed and Breakfast. We were afraid that if he refused Doctor K, he would be harmed to shut him up about the offer, so he made a deal with Doctor K. He would be paid in cash weekly plus a substantial bonus if he came up with something usable. From time to time he produced some harmless notes I had deliberately made. I believe Doctor K became impatient and suspicious and had to get rid of Klaus.

"I don't think I can fill Klaus's shoes," Sven said, but I have many skills.

"We can't expect that of anyone. You've excellent references. We're very satisfied with you and hope you are with us." "Hamid said.

"I wonder who to blame for poisoning me," Cory said.

"You were poisoned?" Hamid shouted.

Allison related the incident that occurred in San Francisco. "Perhaps Doctor K had something to do with that, too. I recall overhearing Klaus speak on his phone that day. He said he had to drop off some pastry at the B and B and had something for him. Klaus was to pick him up in front of our house. Possibly Klaus offered him some pastry from the box and Dr K managed to slip arsenic on the rest of the batch slated for the B and B to incriminate Klaus—to get even with him for not producing any results and to make sure he wouldn't reveal his spying."

"That may explain it." Cory's relief was palpable.

As if to punctuate the happy moment, the sun beamed through the window. Cory gazed out at a clear blue sky. "I'd love to take a walk."

"Let's go for it. Get ready while I make calls," Ben said.

Cory changed into running clothes and waited for Ben. Busy on the phone, he waved as though shooing her off. She was half way out the door when he called, "I'm almost done. Wait or go slowly."

She took her time and headed toward the park, the sun warming her back. The soles of her shoes slid across a tiny patch of slick pavement, but the rest of the sidewalk had begun to dry. She looked over her shoulder and saw Ben jogging toward her. Feeling safe, she took a deep breath and broke into a run.

Crisp air seared her cheeks as she hit her favorite path. Footsteps echoed hers as they struck behind her. She figured they were Ben's. Like a child, she ran faster, wanting him to chase her. Suddenly as the steps drew closer, she sniffed a familiar scent. Paco Rabanne X-S.

In an instant, an arm reached across her throat stifling her scream. She thrust her body forward, tossing the pursuer over her back. Landing face up, his head crashed on the ground. She stared down into the glazed eyes and pained face of Doctor Kami Khatami.

As she leaned over to examine him, he jabbed her in the stomach with his knees. She doubled over and fell on him. He clutched at her throat. She clawed at him with her fingernails and pulled his hands away. With the strength of a mad man, consumed by a goal, he lifted himself, pushing her off. She bounced up. He lunged toward her.

She sidestepped him and kicked high, aiming for his chin. Once again, he fell. Karate gave her the upper hand. She was about to let him have it, when Ben arrived and pulled him up. "Let's go. The police are meeting us outside the park."

Doctor K tried to break loose, but Ben and Cory dragged him along by his arms. Two police cars arrived at the entrance just as they did. An officer cuffed and escorted Doctor Khatami into the vehicle. Cory and Ben accompanied them in another vehicle and headed for the precinct.

After identifying Kami Khatami as the man who had abducted and assaulted her, Cory signed a statement. The officers drove them back to the flat.

"What happened? Allison asked. "We were worried. You were gone so long."

Ben explained the situation. "We're leaving here for San Diego tomorrow morning. Have you made plans?"

"We booked an early morning flight to San Francisco. Sven and Molly are on board, too."

Ah, San Francisco. That's where this all started.

~ ~ ~

About the Author

Sandra L. Ceren, Ph.D. a native New Yorker resides on the California coast. A clinical psychologist for over forty years she is a Diplomate from the American Board of Family Psychology, and Fellow of the Academy of Family Psychology.

She has appeared on *Oprah*, *Good Morning America* and BBC and has reported on mental health research and answered queries in a weekly health column "Ask Dr. Ceren". This popular column was published in newspapers over many years.

A premarital counseling specialist, her books *Essentials Of Premarital Counseling*, addressed to mental health professionals, and *Look Before You Leap-A Premarital Guide For Couples* were published by Loving Healing Press.

Ceren has a passion for writing fiction. *Prescription For Terror*, the first in her series of psychological thrillers featuring a spunky psychologist/sleuth was published in 1999.

Imposter For Hire, book #3 in the Dr. Cory Cohen Mysteries will be followed her next adventure in *2013*.

Over a dozen of her short mystery stories have been published in anthologies and magazines including: *Mystery Magazine*, *Detective Mystery Stories*, and *Criminal Kabbalah*.